"Good N[ight]"

Thanks for an ... *interest[ing]*

He looked disappointed. "Not even a cup of coffee to see me on my way 'cross town?"

"Ask the doorman to phone for a cab."

"I'd hate to wake him up."

"Wake him up."

"You're a pretty tough lady."

She tried to suppress a smile. "You have to be to get along in this town."

He bent over and placed a warm kiss on her lips, his hand resting gently against her neck. For a moment she remained standing with her eyes closed. Then she said, "Casey, tonight had never happened."

"Never. Never happened. I'll try to remember that."

"Tomorrow," she began.

"There'll be no tomorrow. However, there'll be a Saturday. I'll rent the car and come by for you ..." He paused. "When?"

She drew in a deep sigh. "Casey, good night." She went quickly into her apartment, trying to stop herself from wanting him to come in after her. For the second time that night, she closed the door firmly in his smiling face.

Dear Reader,

Welcome to Silhouette! Our goal is to give you hours of unbeatable reading pleasure, and we hope you'll enjoy each month's six new Silhouette Desires. These sensual, provocative love stories are both believable and compelling—sometimes they're poignant, sometimes humorous, but always enjoyable.

Indulge yourself. Experience all the passion and excitement of falling in love along with our heroine as she meets the irresistible man of her dreams and together they overcome all obstacles in the path to a happy ending.

If this is your first Desire, I hope it'll be the first of many. If you're already a Silhouette Desire reader, thanks for your support! Look for some of your favorite authors in the coming months: Stephanie James, Diana Palmer, Dixie Browning, Ann Major and Doreen Owens Malek, to name just a few.

Happy reading!

Isabel Swift
Senior Editor

SDRL-7/85

EVE GLADSTONE
Night Talk

Silhouette Desire

Published by Silhouette Books New York

America's Publisher of Contemporary Romance

SILHOUETTE BOOKS
300 East 42nd St., New York, N.Y.   10017

Copyright © 1986 by Herman Werner & Joyce Gleit

ISBN: 0-373-05284-7

First Silhouette Books printing June 1986

America's Publisher of Contemporary Romance

Printed in the U.S.A.

Books by Eve Gladstone

Silhouette Special Edition

Fortune's Play #78

Silhouette Desire

Ballinger's Rule #108
The Confidence Man #221
Night Talk #284

Silhouette Intimate Moments

Power Play #55
Illusions #138

EVE GLADSTONE

lives in a New York suburb and has published a number of books, both fiction and nonfiction for children, teens and adults. Apart from painting and writing, she's a voracious reader of romance novels.

To Lisa, Jonathan and Stefanie

One

Julie was suddenly aware of Casey Phillips behind her, coming in on tiger's feet. The door to the studio had opened and closed silently, but she could see him reflected in the glass of the darkened control booth. Shirt-sleeves rolled back, hands in his pockets, he was California cool. Only this was New York and the wee hours of a spring morning at WRBZ, 102.1 FM. Tall, sandy-haired Casey Phillips, with clever blue eyes and entirely too much self-confidence.

She didn't turn around but warily watched his approach through the glass, her fingers wrapped tightly around a yellow number-two pencil. She had to restrain herself from splitting it in half. Quite simply he unnerved her. She felt his presence and the unmistakable aura of sensuality that swept into the studio with him with more force than she knew was good for her.

It was unfair, all that power, all that braggadocio and self-confidence wrapped up in such a sexy package. This was the man who wanted her late-night talk show canceled as of yesterday, the man bent upon turning her neat, ordered life upside down. It was only her ironclad contract, with almost a year to go, that kept him from his appointed task.

Brash, abrasive, arrogant. Those were the words whispered about him in the corridors of the station and over the water cooler. She agreed with all of them and had invented a few of her own.

He stopped just behind her chair, his eyes meeting hers in the glass, their reflections superimposed on the shadowy backdrop of the control booth.

Julie wanted to outstare him but couldn't quite manage it, blinking after the passage of a moment or two. There was something new about him, something unexpected. She felt as though she were seeing him for the first time, his reflection softened, his soul bared, as if Casey Phillips was quite human after all.

He shifted slightly under her gaze. The moment of contact was gone and Julie was as uncomfortably aware of his insolent smile as ever, of this formidable opponent, the man who had won every move so far.

He came around, pulled up a chair opposite her, and straddled it. Oh, he was relaxed all right—the informal hatchet man, easygoing and accessible—with the powers, if not the accoutrements, of a third-world dictator.

Without apparent interest, he took in the leavings of the talk show that had just ended: the gray Formica table littered with ashtrays filled to overflowing; coffee containers holding leftover soured coffee; memo pads crisscrossed with angry doodles. To top it off, someone had written her name—Julie Garrett, a heart dotting the *i* in Julie—on the table with a broad felt-tip pen.

He turned silently toward her, his lazy, hooded gaze tracing in the most sensual way her hair, the white collar of her blouse, the bright-red linen suit she wore. Something stubborn in her refused to give ground. She remained very still, feeling his gaze like a delicate, shameless touch against her skin, and allowed a slight smile to play around her lips.

"I'm for vitamin C, myself," he stated at last in a deceptively good-natured manner, although the hint of sarcasm wasn't lost on her. "Among the great issues of the day so vital to the success of your talk show, I'd say the vitamin C proponents won tonight's skirmish. On to the Super Bowl."

"If you paid attention to my show every night instead of searching for reasons to knock it, you'd know that *Night Talk* covers plenty of weighty issues." She had sworn she wouldn't try to defend her program, not to Casey Phillips at any rate. Arguing with the man who was bent on destroying it would only show her fear, but she plunged on anyway. "I try for balance and you know it. My audience is made up of a cross section of the population and—"

"And," he put in, "we always give the public what it clamors for here at WRBZ, music radio."

"Music radio," she sputtered. "Noise radio is more like it. If you had your way, twenty-four hours a day of noise radio." That, of course, was the heart of the matter.

"What does your public clamor for?" he went on lightly. "One night the mind-boggling topic, 'Should Stray Animals Be Neutered?' Last night, if memory serves me, we were all kept on our toes while two cranks argued over whether private or public funds should be used to supply shrubbery along Park Avenue. Public by all means. Then we can use the city's homeless to decorate it all."

She caught a sudden flash of anger in his eyes even as his smile deepened. She kept her gaze steady, however, ignoring the slight flush that was suffusing her cheeks. "My program airs five nights a week, two hours a night," she said with the careful patience of one who has argued the subject before. "Not every subject is to your particular taste, but then why should it be? You're new to the city and you're only interested in destroying its collective hearing with the music you're obviously so addicted to. I suppose you're going to knock the mayor next. He was on last week, fielding telephone calls, *if* you remember."

"With the mayoralty primaries coming up," he remarked, "he'd appear in your refrigerator for fifteen minutes, and not even on prime time."

She was a fool to try to argue with him. He was deliberately goading her and she was responding. Still, on she went, knowing he would try to trip her up. "The week before that the commissioner of transportation was on. Not exactly a lightweight program, but then I don't suppose you know the first thing about public transportation."

"Hearing the commissioner of transportation speak," he said at once, "is preferable only to being out in Lincoln Tunnel at rush hour, which is where the commissioner should be."

"Perhaps," she said evenly, not trusting herself to keep her temper much longer, "you'd like to come on the show, Mr. Station Manager, and have an open discussion of the changes you're making here, and why. Or are you afraid of what my listeners might say?" Since his answer was preordained, Julie was sorry as soon as she had spoken the words.

She put the pencil down and reached for her coffee mug, which only had cold leavings at the bottom and traces of ash from someone's cigarette. Hadn't the vitamin C proponent smoked one cigarette after another? She deliberately put the mug to her mouth and pretended to take a sip, needing the moment to simmer down.

But of course, he was a master of surprise. He leaned closer in his chair, as if knowing what it took to make her uncomfortable, and removed the cup from her hands. Glancing at its contents, he said, "Ah, of course, health food. Great pick-me-up at this time of night. About your proposal." He put the cup down. "I'd be delighted to take you on, but it'd be foolish to bore the pajamas off your tiny band of insomniacs with our private quarrel."

He was close, his breath warm, his eyes holding hers. She watched mesmerized as his lips curled in a slow smile. He knew full well the effect he was having on her. "What say, midnight lady, to our discussing some highly pertinent topics tonight, like how do you take your steaks, rare, medium or very well done? or who's your favorite wrestler? and is the view from my apartment worth the price I'm paying?"

Of course, he couldn't resist propositioning her. It was what every red-blooded male expected every red-blooded female to expect, especially at two in the morning. It all came into focus. Julie picked the pencil up once again, and curled her fingers carefully around it, thinking, must not break it, must not lose one's temper.

"Mr. Phillips, *Casey*," she said, drawing out the words, "I'm sure your sunburned Hollywood charm works like greased lightning with the starlets in your hometown, but we here in the East are used to a more subtle approach."

"I'm a man on the run," he said. "I gave you subtlety a long time ago."

"Then you won't mind my being unsubtle, either. I don't know why you're here—"

"Don't you?"

She caught her breath, then deliberately went on, "It's a little late to be discussing the pros and cons of *Night Talk*, isn't it? I've still got a few things I have to do. I'll be glad to set up an appointment with your secretary for some time tomorrow."

"All work and no play...dull, dull, dull," he said. "I'm not certain why I ankled in here, but it'll come to me." He stood up and with a quick salute, turned and left the studio as silently as he had come. Julie, all the while feeling her face grow warm again with something more than anger, watched his departure through the reflecting glass of the control booth.

Why *had* he come to see her? And why had he left so abruptly? Why had he first baited then propositioned her? And why, in the end, had she wanted him to keep trying? She got to her feet. The hour of the morning, no doubt. She, too, worked long, odd hours to which she had never quite adjusted.

Julie was seldom without verbal resources, but tonight he had managed mentally to twist her arm into silence. Quite a feat, but one that he was clearly up to, with or without sleep.

Casey Phillips had been with WRBZ for two months, eight endless weeks, sixty days, a thousand hours, countless minutes and interminable seconds. From the moment he had taken over the corner office in the executive suite, nothing at the station had been the same. He was the new broom who'd been hired to sweep the WRBZ airwaves clean, and with a vengeance; hired away from a Los Angeles station that he, in the matter of a year, had turned around financially. Casey Phillips was committed to performing the same miracle at WRBZ. His solution, as at his previous job, was to change it to an all-day-all-night rock music station. Music, music, music, and commercials to fill the spaces in between.

Worst of all, there was nothing the man would like better to do than tear up her contract and see the end of Julie Garrett. As she gathered up her notes and her ceramic coffee mug she thought that she had had quite enough of him and his crooked grin and his sarcasm. She fought an almost uncontrollable desire to follow him back into his office just to tell him to get off her back. No more visits to her studio whether she was on or off the air, no more comments about the contents of her show, and no more innuendos about what they might or might not do together after her show.

What in the world was he doing at the station anyway at two in the morning when the night manager was on duty? Did the man never sleep?

As she started down the corridor toward her office she noticed the red light on the door to the studio next to hers. Vic Cooper's jazz program, which preceded her show, was just as iffy as *Night Talk*. They all ought to get together and form their own radio station, she thought. There *were* people out there, and plenty of them, who wanted good music and good talk, and who would support them.

No, she sighed, she didn't know that for sure. She quietly opened the door to the studio. Cooper sat at a huge console, surrounded by the computerized paraphernalia of the engineer's craft. He was a jazz musician who had played trumpet back in the forties with Benny Goodman and had run *Cooper on Jazz* on one radio station or another in different cities, ever since he had quit playing in bands. A member of both the engineers' union and announcers' local, he ran his own program without help from a control room. He spoke into a mike, pushed tapes and discs around, and occasionally interviewed someone.

"Hi, Coop. What are you doing here?" Julie removed a pile of tapes from a worn leather chair, and after putting them on his worktable, sat down. "Don't you ever go home?"

Vic Cooper was bald and gray-bearded, with pale, sleepy eyes that lit up with pleasure when he saw her. "Julie, Julie, Julie, what's doin'?" he said, not bothering to answer her question. He often hung around the station after hours going through his huge, valuable old record collection.

"Trying to work up a good steam is what's doin'," she said.

"Tell Poppa your problems. Is it love?" he asked. "Do you have money worries? Acid indigestion? Don't know what to do with your two weeks' vacation? Poppa Cooper advises on all and sundry problems."

"This problem," Julie said, laughing, "is known as Casey Phillips. Symptoms? A certain feeling of arrogance in the upper cranial region. A know-it-all bump that grows out of the left lobe. The kind of illness that produces in others a change of life known as, eek, the station's been sold down the river, what do we do now? Oh, and diagnosis: form your own radio station and the devil with him."

"I get the impression you don't like the man."

"Really?" said Julie. "Funny, I didn't mean it to read that way."

Cooper reached over and patted her hand. "He's in over his head, lovely one. He thinks the East coast is the West coast, only with four seasons. He'll find the ratings will plummet, and so will his career."

"And in the meantime?"

"In the meantime, wait it out. If worse comes to worst, we'll find our collective way to other stations."

"It won't be that easy, Coop. You know it," she said tiredly.

"It's a big AM—FM world out there. Cable radio is the hottest new thing, anyway. Who needs this local stuff? Get yourself syndicated."

"That easy, huh?"

"You haven't tried." Coop leaned forward and fiddled aimlessly with a couple of dials. "You're a looker. You could also bring your case to one of the television stations."

"A looker," she quoted, automatically raising a hand to her short, brown hair. "That's a fine howdy-do when I begin to cash in on that, and not on my ability."

"Can't hurt."

Julie wondered. She had high cheekbones and heavy-lidded dark eyes that the camera caressed. A looker? Maybe. Not beautiful, certainly. It was a matter of basic bone structure and nothing more. Genes, that was all. A little different, however, from the genes that had got her a scholarship to study journalism, brought her prestigious newspaper jobs, and at last delivered her to WRBZ.

Television. It was not the first time the idea had been mentioned. Her agent had told her it was a possibility but, when Julie pressed the issue, he admitted that the most he would be able to do for her would be a capsule appearance on someone else's show, perhaps one or two days a week.

After that night's contretemps with Casey Phillips however, the possibility began to look good. Even a capsule appearance on a show would bring her the same income as her five nights a week radio program. She decided to call her agent about it in the morning, and about cable syndication.

"See you, Coop," she said, getting up.

"Smile," he told her. "You're on your way to the top, kid."

She walked thoughtfully to her office, a room at the back of the tall building on Fifth Avenue that housed the radio station. It was a tiny, windowless shell that she shared with her assistant, Sara Lowry. There were two desks—Sara's against the wall, hers facing the door—both covered with books, papers and piles of correspondence. Philodendron plants were doing well under the fluorescent light, a fat teddy bear with one bent ear sat on the file cabinet, and a huge poster of a muscle-bound movie star hung crookedly on the wall by Sara's desk; the office was tiny, but it was home and sacred territory.

Sara had waved at Julie after the broadcast, and left at once to escort the night's guests to their cabs. Sara and she would meet again at four the following day to brief themselves on the backgrounds of the evening's guests and to prepare the questions that Julie would put to them.

Julie closed the door to her office. All at once she felt a wave of claustrophobia engulf her. She fought a desire to pull the door open again, deciding that she needed the privacy. She didn't want anybody dropping in on her, not tonight, not after that odd and unsatisfactory meeting with Casey Phillips.

She needed time to think, to map out some sort of strategy for dealing with him. Yet even now, with her anger quietly smoldering, she could clearly remember the tingle along her spine when those magnetic blue eyes had raked over her body so insolently. Going behind her desk, she sat down and put her hands behind her head, staring at the ceiling with its white, crackled oblongs of pressboard. A sudden longing came over her that was so intense she felt she could gather it in her hands.

A longing for what? Julie wondered. For change? But she was resisting change, trying to shut out the possibility. Or was it the accumulation of events missed? Of coming back to her empty apartment; of relationships and friendships not pursued; of a shallowness she seemed to cultivate when she was off the air?

She thought with an awful surprise that there was really no one, no one at all that she was attached to or who had really touched her life. Not even her sister counted, nor her niece, Lindy, just turned sixteen, both living the good suburban life in Stamford, Connecticut. Their life-style was too remote, too insular. Her sister was six years her senior, and they had never shared their youth.

No, there was no one. In fact Julie wore the kind of facade that anyone who has achieved a certain public success might wear. Only she knew it was a cover-up, one-dimensional, in spite of the depth she needed for *Night Talk*.

She laughed lightly. It was a good thing she'd never had a program with women like herself discussing their problems. There was no way she could have been an objective host.

Why had she avoided personal contacts? She was thirty years old; she'd had a couple of love affairs in the past that she knew from the beginning wouldn't turn into anything. She had simply kept life at a distance.

Julie knew deep in her heart that she wanted the basics in life. She wanted somebody to lie in bed with and read the paper on Sunday mornings; someone to send out for Chinese food with. She wanted a simple relationship in which she could relax and have fun and wear a pair of torn jeans and watch late movies on television.

Good heavens, she said to herself, what in the world was she thinking about at two in the morning? Why would her argument with Casey Phillips trigger such sentimentality, such longing?

Perhaps it was merely because she was uncertain how to tackle the man. In the back of her mind, ready to upset all her preconceived notions, was the memory of that odd moment of contact back there in the studio. The other Casey Phillips, viewed through a glass not at all darkly. Did he exist or had she conjured him up? Wishful thinking, perhaps. If only he had come on a white charger to save the station instead of assisting in its downfall!

In some ways, the sale of WRBZ to the Graff Corporation had come as no surprise. It had been an anomaly among New York radio stations. It was commercial but with quirky, interesting programming that was not available through other outlets. As a result, the steady, small audience consisted of people with a wide range of ages and interests: teenagers, artists, lawyers, retirees; an unspecialized audience that advertisers steered clear of.

When the announcement of the sale to Graff had been made, station personnel had been told that the new owners would make no immediate changes. A general sigh of relief wafted down the corridors and through the studios. However within the month the previous station manager, who had been a part-owner of WRBZ, was gone, Casey had been hired, and everything was suddenly turned upside down. Change began in earnest.

The art deco skyscraper that housed the radio station was purchased by Graff Corporation, which among other things made computer hardware. Painting and renovation of the executive offices and radio station began at once.

Phillips, the staff learned as soon as he was installed in the handsome corner office on the forty-ninth floor of the building, had no interest in loyalty or length of service with the station. His god was the bottom line, profit and loss, loss and profit, and that was that.

The general trembling had begun when Phillips announced his draconian plans for WRBZ; his threats would not abate, Julie supposed, until every last one of the old guard was gone. Well, she was going to hang in there. Tenacious Julie Garrett, they had called her back home in Brookline, Massachusetts.

A note on yellow legal paper was placed squarely on top of her typewriter; Sara's bold handwriting leaped out at her:

> Need a chit for the limousine on Monday. Opie Hart wants the Famous Designer treatment, and the Big Boss wants everything in sextuplicate. And I do mean sex!

Julie drew her fingers through her hair and let out a sigh that seemed to echo around the office. Vitamin C today, and tomorrow—Opie Hart, a dress designer with a dreadfully phony Spanish accent. He was married to a pretender to the throne of Saxony and billed himself as "the couturier to royalty." Quite entertaining but, viewed in the light of Casey Phillips's remarks, inviting Opie Hart to talk about his silk-lined jeans had been a tactical mistake.

She made a quick mental run-through of the rest of the guests who were scheduled for the week. A man who gave permanents to show dogs. A bag lady who talked quite lucidly about her plight, if they could find her. A panel of popular genre writers. Good Lord, it was one of those weeks again. She hadn't been able to line up any labor leaders or important politicians, or anyone with an ecological ax to grind. The rest of the week promised to be wall-to-wall fluff, the kind that was impossible to vacuum up. Damn.

Casey Phillips was moving in fast. He wanted that time slot and would love to see her off the air before her contract was due for renewal.

Sara had left her several more messages. Her sister had called with a reminder to bring the pesto sauce for Saturday night. She thought about calling up one of the men she dated to go with her, but couldn't make up her mind. It would be easier all around to make the sauce, catch a train up, stay overnight and come back on Sunday. She could have a nice visit with her sister and niece while she was at it. *Make an effort, Julie,* she told herself. It's time to get close.

There were also two apparently urgent messages from someone she had met at a cocktail party, an expert on Edgar Allen Poe who wrote and published an illiterate newsletter on the subject. Her lawyer had called. The other messages were from listeners whose names she either did not know, or did know because they called nightly with suggestions or complaints.

Last of all, in Sara's handwriting, now turned spidery and secret, was a note that Julie furiously crumpled into a ball after reading:

Casey Phillips was here when I came back from the studio. Just *browsing*, he said.

The nerve, thought Julie, taking the ball of paper and throwing it across the room. He's snooping. *Snooping.* Attrition, that's what it's all about. He won't try to break my contract; he just wants to wear me down.

She considered calling her lawyer to find out whether or not they could legally force him to keep away from her. No, she was a big girl now, and the last thing she wanted to do was shove her contract under Phillips's nose. Words, reasonably stated, eye-to-eye contact, at once, while she was still steaming.

It was twenty past two when Julie reached for the telephone and started to dial Casey Phillips's extension. Then she thought better of it. Surprise was a far better tactic. She grabbed her bag, locked up and went firmly down the quiet corridor toward the executive suite at the front of the building. She might as well get it over with now, while her anger was still high. Tomorrow he would think of something new, leaving her stuttering in surprise.

The station, on air twenty-four hours a day, was always brightly lit. At night, however, because there was scarcely anyone around, the atmosphere was vaguely eerie and disquieting. Julie felt it particularly so that night, as she hurried along, trying to figure how she would handle Phillips.

He needed some education about the work that was accomplished by socially responsible programs such as hers. He also needed to be taught that it wasn't always possible to ante up a stellar cast every night. Besides, her listeners preferred variety. Tragedy and comedy, just like life.

The measures Casey Phillips had taken to change the station programming had been swift and merciless; the staff was still reeling from them. Some had already departed, some had had their positions improved, and others, like Julie, had only their contracts to hold on to.

The executive suite was a contrast to the broadcasting offices at the back of the building where quiet, functional materials had been used, and there was a workaday quality. Here all was heavy wool carpeting, wool tweed wall coverings, and no-expense-spared.

A uniformed guard was on duty as she walked through the reception room. She smiled at him. "Mr. Phillips still in?" Rock music played through loudspeakers that were on all day; visitors in the waiting room were always treated to the current program.

"Far as I know," the guard said.

"I'm on my way, then."

The station manager's corner office was down a carpeted corridor. It had wraparound windows with a downtown view of the city and the Empire State Building.

When Julie walked into the outer office, the quiet hit her in spite of the ever-present background music. The mahogany door to Phillips's office was closed and Julie, with an unexpected feeling of disappointment that had nothing to do with why she was there, wondered whether Casey had gone home. She paused and then went swiftly over to his door and tapped lightly on it. Receiving no answer, she reached for the handle and pushed it open.

She found Casey Phillips leaning back in his chair, framed by the wide view of the city lights beyond, long legs crossed on the desktop, hands clasped behind his head.

"I knew it was you," he said at once, with a wry smile.

Loudspeakers placed strategically around the office ground out the same rock music as in the reception room, but the sound was turned so low that even the heavy beat was lost. Julie had the sudden, uncomfortable feeling of having walked into a trap.

"I'd like a word with you," she stated truculently, coming briskly across the thick sienna carpet.

"You're ready to explode," he said. "Go ahead. It'll clear the air."

He was maneuvering, trying to put her on the defensive, but Julie wasn't buying. She leaned forward and rested her hands on his desk. "I'm not about to explode at all," she said in her most reasonable tone. "I've come to have a quiet discussion with you."

"Discuss away."

"As easy as that." After the briefest hesitation, she pulled a chair up to the desk and sat down.

"Have a seat," he said.

"Thank you. You're so kind." She waited for a moment—not to compose herself but perversely to add to the general atmosphere of cat and mouse that he seemed to be creating. Which of them would be the cat and which the mouse in the long run? she wondered.

"Your quiet discussion," he prompted.

Julie had learned early that being a talk show host had many benefits, one of which was learning to turn any situation to her advantage. She met his gaze directly. "I realize that your attention span for shows like mine is limited. For women who want to talk to you about something serious it's even shorter, I imagine. But if you'll bear with me?"

"I'm bearing with you, difficult as that may be. In fact," he said, "I'm all attention. Just as I was this evening when that stimulating discussion on vitamin C was burning up the airwaves."

"I think all that hard rock noise has rattled your brains, Mr. Phillips."

"I doubt it," he remarked, "since I never listen to it."

"Oh, I see," she said, scarcely trying to hide her exasperation, "you don't care what the station plays, as long as you can keep ringing up the cash register. I don't think that's what radio was meant for."

"And you've a direct connection to the Keeper of the Airwaves, I suppose, who told you that rock music is bad, violin music is good, and vitamin C is particularly good. Frankly, Garrett, I don't buy that. Now why, exactly, are you here?"

"I'll make it brief," she said, "so even you'll understand. One, for the length of my contract, stay out of my studio. Two, for the length of my contract, I'll see you in *your* office if there's business to discuss, such as renewing my contract, and three, stop knocking what I do for a living when we *do* meet." He raised his hands in a gesture of surrender, but Julie hurried on. "And four—"

"Uh-uh," he told her, smiling, "three's my limit. Four is taking advantage of my good nature."

"And four," she went on, not paying the slightest attention to him, "we chauffeur our guests to and fro and I hope we won't have to beg for measly cab fare. On occasion, we're even going to have to hire a limousine and WRBZ is going to cough up for it. And you want copies of the chit in sextuplicate, which is all part of your attempt to make me lose my temper and tear up my contract. Mr. Phillips," she said, standing up and going over to his desk, then leaning on her fists, her face inches from his, "I never lose my temper."

"Too bad your program isn't televised," he commented dryly. His glance, quick and knowledgeable, swept over every inch of her body. "That fire in your eyes would knock your audience dead every time."

"Good night, Casey-ever-at-the-bat." She turned and went quickly toward the door, only to find him moving in on her. In another moment he had placed his hand over hers to prevent her from opening the door.

"Would you mind?" She ground out the words angrily, trying to pull away from his warm touch. His hands, she noted almost inadvertently, were well shaped with long, slender fingers.

"Let's talk about it," he said in a suddenly cajoling tone, releasing her hand. "I admit that maybe I did come on a bit strong back there in the studio, but believe it or not I was seeing a really attractive woman, one I wanted to spend time with, and it had nothing to do with your show. If I have a gripe, it's about the program, not you."

She gave an impatient sigh. "If you think that *Night Talk* and I are separate, you're wrong. My advice to you in the love-your-neighbor department is that you need a soul to begin with, Mr. Businessman. What you have, apparently, is made of highly polished and cut zirconium, and not the genuine article at all. Now, if you don't mind." She reached for the door once again and jerked it open, aware both that her heart was beating rapidly and that this exasperating, incorrigible man was entirely too attractive and clever. She turned to him with blazing eyes. "I said it and I mean it. Stay out of my hair."

"Strange," he said with a crooked grin. "That's just the place I'd like to find myself."

For a moment Julie stood there, letting the anger drive through her. Then she turned around quickly and left his office. As a last gesture, with all the force she could muster, she slammed the door in his face.

Two

___

Julie jabbed the elevator button impatiently, tracking the elevator's descent. She had a feeling that Casey might try to follow her. Just as it slid to a halt and the door opened, Vic Cooper came running up.

"Hey," he said, "long time no see."

"Ten minutes," Julie remarked as the door closed behind them and she could breathe a sigh of relief.

With a second look at her expression, Coop said, "That bad, huh?"

"He's incorrigible. Anyway, I got my licks in, Coop. You'd have been proud of me. I told him to stay out of my hair." She stopped abruptly, remembering his response.

"You look as if you need a tall, cool drink. I'm on my way to Harris's," he said, referring to a well-known jazz club on West Fifty-second Street. "Come on, kid, buy you one."

"No thanks, Vic. I'd better head home."

"Steaming ain't good when you're all alone," he said, singing the words as though they were part of a lyric.

She closed her eyes briefly. When the elevator slid to a halt at the lobby floor she had made up her mind. Jazz would be just the thing for getting rid of the Casey Phillips blues. "Sure. For a while, anyway, Vic." She slipped her arm through his. "Let's go."

The band was playing "Sweet Georgia Brown" in an irrepressible New Orleans style when they came into the smoky, crowded club. The owner himself came forward to greet them, a smiling man in a well-cut business suit.

"Hey, Vic, it's about time you showed up, you old ringer. Where've you been?" He glanced at Julie with bright, appraising eyes.

"Julie Garrett, Ben Harris," Vic said.

Harris encased Julie's hand in a warm, friendly shake, just as the piece ended. There was enthusiastic applause from the crowd. On the bandstand, which was in the center of the long, narrow club, she saw the trumpeter draw over the mike. "And now," he announced in a low, pleasant croon, "here's my other favorite girl, 'Little Liza Jane.'"

Harris led them to seats opposite the bandstand. A long, worn leather-cushioned banquette ran the length of the wall beneath a montage of black and white photographs. Portraits of jazz musicians and singers had been pasted down haphazardly and were yellowed with age. It was the music that counted here, she reflected, not the ambience. Julie slid into the banquette and Vic took a seat opposite her, so that he had to turn to watch the band play.

The set ended. The musicians put down their instruments and stretched. Some customers got up reluctantly and sauntered out; others came in and took their places.

The trumpeter, still in his seat on the bandstand, called out to Vic. "Hey, Vic, how are ya, man? We were just talking about you."

"Okay, Joe, you? Been busy."

Julie, waiting for the beer Vic had ordered, listened lazily to the talk. Casey was still on her mind and she wondered whether she'd had the last word after all. So intent was she on her thoughts, that she didn't even glance at the shadow that fell across their table until she heard Coop's chair scrape back on the wooden floor. The next thing she knew, Coop was on his feet pumping Casey Phillips's hand vigorously.

Casey looked down at Julie with a curious glint in his eyes.

"Hey, come on, join us," Coop invited him.

"Please," said Julie, fanning out her hand. "Don't let me stop you."

Casey grinned and sat down next to her on the banquette. "Imagine my surprise," he began and then laughed.

"I'll just bet," she said.

They were joined in another moment by the pianist, Sammy Roy, who turned a curious eye on Julie. "Where do I know you from?" he asked when Coop introduced them.

"I've come here before," she said.

"Yeah, but Garrett, Julie Garrett."

"*Night Talk,*" Casey said with a show of impatience. "She runs a program on WRBZ."

"That's it, that's it," he said, slapping the table enthusiastically. "I listen when I'm between gigs. It comes on after *Cooper and Jazz.* Hey, nice to know you. Well, well." He reached out and shook her hand. He turned to

Casey. "Come up later, show the little lady what you can do."

He left, giving Julie a lingering smile.

"Oh, the pleasure of fame," she said. "Can you imagine, I have a real, live listener. What does he mean, show the little lady what you can do? Casey, I *know* what you can do."

"Do you now?"

"Confession time, Case. For a man hell-bent on turning the station into a rock nightmare, you'll have to explain Sammy's last remark. Back flips? Trumpet? Piano? Kazoo? All explanations cheerfully accepted. Coop, do you know?"

"Ask him," Coop said, turning away and feigning indifference.

Casey reached for a book of matches and opened it carefully. She watched as he bent a match and set it aflame between cupped fingers. Beautiful hands with long, sensitive fingers. She knew before he said the word. The light flickered against his face, lending it angled shadows that gave it a surprising depth of character. He lit the candle that sat on the table in a tiny red glass holder—a tentative flame that cast a faint, rosy hue.

"I thought you knew I played piano," he said.

"Why would I know that?" She felt a strange sensation in the region of her heart, as though she were about to learn something she didn't want to know, something good that might endear Casey to her.

"If you don't, you've got a lot of catching up to do," he was saying.

"About your piano playing?" she asked.

"No, about me."

"Now why would I want to do that? We're sworn enemies, remember? How come piano? How come jazz? It is
jazz, isn't it? You're a bundle of contradictions, Casey."

"You'll find that I'm a real easy read, Julie, if you just
come out from behind those blinders you put on when it
comes to one Casey Phillips. How come piano?" He
smiled as if genuinely glad that she showed interest in him.
"My mother made me practice. She really thought I'd get
to Carnegie Hall."

His beer arrived and he picked up the glass at once,
taking a long draft. Julie hadn't touched hers. She put her
chin in her hand and turned toward him. "Somehow I
didn't quite match you with a mother. Amazing. Tell me
everything."

"Oh, I had one of those and more," he said. "I had a
father, too. Several of those. Casey Phillips Senior was—
is—a movie producer and my mother *was* an aspiring ac-
tress. They got married, had me, and then divorced. Once
they were in the marrying mood they went through the
routine a couple of times more—each. I shuttled back and
forth between their respective households until I tired of
it." He gave a sudden laugh that held something hollow in
it. "The only constant in my life was music."

She put her hand out in an involuntary gesture and
touched his. "I'm sorry, Casey."

"Don't let it get you down. Life in Beverly Hills wasn't
too hard to take. All the accoutrements of money you
didn't work for make life a breeze."

"I suppose they do." She reflected on the difference between that kind of life and the one she had led as a teenager in Brookline. Her mother worked as housekeeper for
an affluent family, and Julie had grown up surrounded by
someone else's wealth.

"Hollywood brat. I think that's the generic term for what I was until I got my act together." He took her hand in his and turned it palm up. "Parties, drinking, good-time friends, fun, until I decided I wanted something more."

"Like the rearranging of priorities at radio stations."

Casey gave her a long, searching look. "That, my friend, came a long time after." He traced the outline of each finger. "Beautiful hands that have never known a day's honest labor," he commented.

She burst out laughing, but nevertheless snatched her hand away. "How little we both know. Good for slapping faces, by the way."

"Touché. Want to tell me about the hard times in Brookline, Massachusetts?"

She was surprised that he knew where she came from, but merely shook her head. She wasn't interested in being a study in contrasts. He had turned toward the bandstand, watching intently as Joe pulled out his trumpet and put it testingly to his lips. Julie leaned back against the banquette and studied Casey's profile. Somewhere between the studio and the club he had lost that driving quality that put her back up and for a moment she wished that Coop would leave so she could be alone with him.

Coop turned to her. "Another beer, Julie?"

She shook her head and watched as he ordered another for himself. The next set had begun and the music, "St. James Infirmary," blasted away any further possibility of conversation.

Pianist. Jazz. Son of a Hollywood producer. But, of course, the latter had been whispered around the station, along with nods of understanding; *how else do you think he got the job?*

With the ending of "St. James," and after the applause had died down, Joe took the microphone in hand. "Our pianist, Sammy Roy, wants a word with you."

"We've a treat for you tonight, folks," Sammy said into the mike. "Where I come from, there's a well-founded notion that some of the best jazz musicians took the wrong road and wound up at the other end of town. You know, the end with the fancy buildings and fancier folk, leaving the likes of us to bring the message to you." He grinned over at Casey. "We've got one of them here tonight, and with a bit of prodding maybe we can coax him up here. Folks, I mean Casey Phillips."

A scattering of applause was accompanied by some bright smiles of recognition.

Casey raised his hands. "Not tonight, Sammy. It's been a long day." He looked quickly at Julie, giving her a slight smile.

"Go ahead, Case," she said. "I'm really curious."

"Is that a dare?"

"I think that's what they call it."

He gave her a sudden, boyish grin and as if he were showing off especially for her, got up and hopped onto the bandstand.

Casey conferred with Joe for a moment. "Goin' It Alone" was announced.

"All right," Coop said, applauding. He turned to Julie and added, "He wrote that, you know."

She shook her head slowly. No, she didn't know. There was a lot about the man she would have to catch up on, that much was certain.

Casey's fingers touched the keyboard, and Julie felt a sudden chill run up her spine at the first notes. She knew at once his music making had that warm, dreamy elegance that separates the ordinary from the exceptional.

The audience felt it, too. The murmur of voices stopped as though they had taken a collective breath and held it.

Coop leaned across the table. "A real comer ten years ago," he said. "And then, poof, just like that, he drops it. Said he was tired of life on the road, that he was tired of hotel rooms and one-night stands and no more dough."

"You knew this all the time," she said, frowning at him.

"What difference does it make? He's doing a number on the station, that's all I know."

"You should have told me."

Coop shrugged and took another swig of his beer. She turned back. The song, which she remembered from a decade before, flowed effortlessly at Casey's touch. His body, gracefully poised over the keys, seemed totally at home with the sounds he was making.

He had taken off his jacket and loosened his tie. A lock of hair had fallen over his forehead, giving him an endearing, vulnerable look. It was as if he had come back to a place he loved.

That inexplicable sense of longing and need came over Julie once again. It was both painful and exquisite and she had a sudden vision of Casey as a boy: a surfer, sun-bronzed with an easy smile, and an even easier manner. He must have wowed them in Beverly Hills. She wondered how much of his charm was real, how much faked; how much of the laid-back look was put on and at what cost.

She'd have to be very careful with him, of that she was certain. He was a man who could set a trap and then stand back to watch without a twitch of a muscle as his prey struggled against the iron clamps. It was difficult, however, to reconcile the hard-driving station manager with the man now before her, charming an audience with grace and talent. She'd never met anyone like him and the trouble was she was reacting to his blatant sexuality like a schoolgirl. Watch it, a tiny voice said, this is a railroad crossing. There could be a monumental collision.

She watched his hands moving with such authority. He would caress a woman's body the same way, knowing, as surely as he knew the notes that awoke at his touch, just how to make her come alive.

Julie shook herself lightly as if to chase away the almost palpable feel of his hands. She could sign her death warrant at the station if she allowed anything to develop between them, but she still couldn't take her eyes away. He held her mesmerized and when he looked up and turned toward her, he caught her eye and winked. A moment later the piece ended. She applauded enthusiastically with the rest of the audience. Sammy whistled and called for an encore, but Casey was already on his feet jumping off the stand.

When Casey came over to the table, his face damp with perspiration, he gave Julie a smile that held something both sheepish and triumphant in it.

"Good man," Vic Cooper said, offering him a sleepy grin.

Casey sat down next to Julie and immediately poured some of the warming beer from the bottle into his glass. He took a long drink before beckoning for refills. Julie pushed her own half-finished glass toward him, and he rewarded her with a smile as he downed it.

"Now that we know you're a closet pianist," she said, "why are you at WRBZ?"

He put his fingers to his lips to silence her and it wasn't until the set was over that he turned back. "'Caravan,'" he said at last, referring to the music the band had just played.

All through the piece, the question had been sitting there, waiting to be answered. Julie didn't give him time to change the subject, wondering at his reluctance to talk about himself. "Casey, you haven't answered my question. Why did you give up jazz for WRBZ?"

"A man's got to do what a man's got to do."

"Ouch. Only Clint Eastwood gets away with a line like that. I just heard an excellent piano player with a beautiful technique."

"I quit while I was ahead," he said simply.

"Really! I'd like to have heard you when you were behind."

He gazed at her, his expression serious. "The world of a musician is pretty upside down," he began.

She nodded, smiling. "Late hours, things like that. It has a vaguely familiar ring to it."

"Okay, Garrett, but there's another side to being a musician, a narcissistic side, self-indulgent and ultimately lonely. I was in a band and we hit more towns in a month than an advancing army. I was always saying goodbye to people I wanted to spend time with, and saying hello to people I never gave a damn about. It was a crazy, cloistered existence in a way. I never knew what the hell was going on in the world. There was one long period—two years, I think—when I didn't pick up a newspaper or book. Two years, when the only print I read was on my contract."

"I remember when everybody on campus was singing 'Goin' It Alone.' You must have had the world by a string, Casey. So far I'm not feeling sorry for you."

"There was 'Goin' It Alone' but there were also a dozen others no one sang, except yours truly. Julie, I loved the music, loved writing it and playing it, and yet I hated it and knew that ultimately, I was nowhere. I was just a kid who wasn't plugged into the real world. I quit one day, just like that. Out in Indiana somewhere. Quit, went back to school and came up for air two years later with an M.B.A.''

"Then on to conquer the broadcasting world as a child prodigy.'' She paused, toying with the idea of not saying any more, then plunged right on. "Or was it all a matter of having the right connections rather than the right stuff?''

He laughed. "You couldn't resist the dig, could you, Garrett? The right connections, of course. I believe in fast starts. What you do once you're cruising down the fairway is something else.''

"You cruised right into the big time.'' The waiter came with a cold beer. She ran her fingers down the length of her glass. "I'm impressed. It's been that kind of night all around.'' She was longing to talk about that other side of him—the side that animated him—the side he apparently thought he had abandoned.

"Big time, all right,'' Coop said. He took a long pull at his beer, and Julie looked across at him.

He was sleepy-eyed and ready for bed, but she knew him, knew he would hang on for all hours unless she sent him home in a cab. Casey gestured to the waiter and asked for the bill. After he had paid, he said, "Come on, Coop, we're going to pour you into a cab and send you off home.'' He got up and led the way out of the club. Julie, following him, smiled. Coop was sleepy all right, and maybe a little drunk. She was glad Casey was there to help with the pouring. Vic Cooper lived in Greenwich Village, and after they disposed of him, she would grab a cab uptown and home.

Once they were out on the street, they found that getting a cab wasn't going to be easy at that hour. When one finally came along, Vic Cooper bowed low and swept an arm toward the cab. "You take the cab, milady. I'll get the next."

"You first, Coop," Julie said. "I can take care of myself."

"In you go, pal," Casey said, taking the disc jockey by the arm and firmly pushing him through the open door into the cab. When it swung away, he stood with Julie at the curbside.

"Let's see, you're upper West Side, I'm upper East Side. I'll drop you off and continue on my way."

There was no cab in sight and for a while it seemed a moot point. "There's always the subway," Casey said.

The air was soft and the moon sent eerie shafts of light into the quiet street. "I actually wouldn't mind walking," Julie said in a tentative voice. "It's just about a mile up Broadway." It was an invitation to Casey to join her and she waited for the knowing grin she was certain he would give her.

Instead he nodded and took her arm. "Suits me. Nothing like a walk up Broadway with a beautiful woman at three in the morning. That's what the Big Apple's all about, isn't it?"

"If you say so, sir." They were silent for a long while after that. The city, which never ceased humming, never shut off completely, at that hour had a waiting, patient air. Midtown Manhattan in the wee hours of the morning was a forest of high-rise buildings buttressed against the low, scudding clouds with lights twinkling on odd floors as cleaning staffs removed the trash of the day.

Julie thought with an inward sigh that she hadn't felt so content in a long time. That she should be ambling homeward with her sworn enemy didn't bear looking into. For the moment it was enough to match his stride as they left block after block behind them, their footsteps part of the faint city sounds. A lone jogger in tight shorts and a sweatband around his head sprinted by, nodding at them, his radio plugged into his ears.

"Some of your horrible music, I suppose," Julie said, "that you never listen to."

"At least you know why."

"Which makes you a snake in the grass."

"Is that what they call earning a living?"

"We're beginning to argue," she said. "What a pity. Just when I was beginning to feel so good."

His hand was still on her arm, his touch gentle. Their bodies, close together, moved in unison. "So you should— feel good, that is. You're with me, safe and sound at three in the morning. Does your mother know you're out, Juliet?"

"She thinks I have a little sense, which I obviously don't."

He smiled. "Maybe that's a good thing, at least from my point of view."

He pulled her around and before she could object, his lips came down on hers. He held her close, his long legs hard against hers. She didn't move when his hands slid from her shoulders to her waist, his lips warm and urgent. When the first reluctant tremor of response stirred in her, he stepped away. "One of us had better," he said, looking smilingly down at her. Then he tucked his arm through hers and drew her along.

"Had better what?" She was getting dense, she thought. Or too sleepy. She had wanted that kiss, there in the middle of the street at that impossible hour with joggers and haunted cats as lookers-on. She had wanted it never to end.

"Had better have a little sense," he told her. "We're two wide-awake people alone in the sleeping universe, Juliet. The stars are fading and dawn will be here before you know it. I can think of a lot of things I'd like to do but there's Saturday, isn't there? What is it? A picnic? Do you make the pesto sauce yourself, or can I pick it up at my favorite Park Avenue deli?''

''My what?'' Her pesto sauce. He had been in her office and had read the note from her sister:

Come Saturday and bring the pesto sauce.

She turned to him, laughing to hide her indignation. ''Are you crazy? You don't mind at all admitting you were in my office reading my phone messages. Then you have the absolute gall to invite yourself along to my sister's house. How do you know I don't already have a date?''

He gave her a patient smile, as though she would shout herself quiet. ''You'll tell me if you do, by and by.''

''I don't have to tell you anything. No, Casey, no, a thousand times no. Tonight was an anomaly. You know, a fluke? A once in a lifetime event? You caught me at a bad time, no a *good* time. But,'' she added, ''to make a poem, also the last time.''

''That's not precisely what I'd call a poem.''

They had stopped at a crosswalk. Three more blocks and they would be at Seventy-third and Broadway. Home. It was crazy. Foolish, dumb. She wanted both to be with him and to get him out of her life forever. ''Casey,'' she said at last. ''Help me. Just go away. Tomorrow is Friday. Work resumed. This unexpected event—our bumping into one another—never happened. I know nothing about you; you know nothing about me...''

''Ah, but that's the trouble,'' he said.

The light turned green. No traffic had passed in either direction, but they had waited obediently for the light to change, for the Walk sign to come on. They were dragging their feet, she thought. Both of them. Oh, he was an enigma, all right. A dangerous enigma.

She began to walk faster. "Casey, the party's over. I've no intention of reading you my past history," she said when he caught up to her.

"Where did you say your sister lives?"

"Damn it, in Stamford, Connecticut, in a big white house surrounded by maples and rhododendron bushes. Undoubtedly the azaleas are in bloom. You're incorrigible and I'm not going to put up with it."

Her apartment building loomed across the way—the Ansonia. It was an elegant old hotel and the sight of it, as always, gave her a feeling of surprise and happiness.

She had been lucky to land the apartment on the seventeenth floor that overlooked downtown Manhattan and New Jersey beyond the Hudson River. The rent was steep. Steps were being taken to turn it into a cooperative apartment house, but she had rented in a flush of exuberance. She had had faith in the success of her program, but now she might be stuck with a rent she couldn't afford if Casey Phillips had his way.

"Home," she told him, crossing the street at a near run.

"Nice."

She pushed open the huge glass door that led into the lobby, which was empty except for the man at the reception desk. He had nodded off and even Julie's heels clicking on the marble floor didn't stir him.

"End of the line," she said to Casey as she hit the elevator button.

"I make deliveries right to the door," he said. "Especially when you can count on the resident gendarme like that," he added, referring to the man asleep at the reception desk.

They were silent in the elevator. Casey was leaning back against the wall, his arms folded across his chest, smiling lazily at her all the way up. She noted, with surprise, that his face was worn and tired. She had the unexpected notion that his job at the station was a lot harder than he made out. They were pressuring him, she thought, and he can't unwind. Well, it was no affair of hers. You take the job, you take the knocks.

At the door to her apartment, she fished around for her keys and then held them up. "The red one for the lower lock, the blue for the upper lock."

He took them and was exaggeratedly careful about opening the door. Then, pushing it to, he stood aside for her to enter.

"The keys, Casey," she said without budging.

He smiled and handed them to her. "Amazing how a man forgets a little thing like that."

"Good night, Casey. Thanks for an...*interesting* time."

He assumed a look of disappointment. "Not even a cup of coffee to see me on my way 'cross town?"

"Ask the receptionist to phone for a cab," she said.

"I'd hate to wake him up."

"Wake him up."

"You're a pretty tough lady."

She tried to suppress a smile. "You have to be to get along in this town."

He bent over and placed a warm kiss on her lips, his hand resting gently against her neck. For a moment she remained standing with her eyes closed even when she knew he had pulled reluctantly away. Then she said, "Casey, tonight never happened."

"Never. Never happened. I'll try to remember that."

"Tomorrow," she began.

Three

It was true. She didn't see Casey on Friday. Sara announced the fact at once when she came in. "Notice the calm, quiet air about the place? Something's wrong with the transmitter and Casey Phillips has been out of the office all day."

The relief of not having to deal with him flowed smoothly over her. "Marvelous," she said gaily. "You're absolutely right. The sun's shining."

Yet there was something else, something that made her cheeks grow unaccountably warm thinking about it. She had wanted to see Casey, had wanted confrontation. She had even worked out the scene in her mind. It would have been in the corridor, Casey rushing in one direction, Julie in the other. He would have grabbed her arm, forced her to stop. She would have been frantically busy and objected. He would have attempted a kiss....

Foolish. Life planned things quite differently. Transmitters had trouble with great regularity all over the world. Julie went over to her desk and sifted through her messages. At four o'clock that morning after she had closed the door on Casey she had tumbled into bed and, contrary to expectations, fallen asleep at once. The blameless sleep of the happy, she supposed. And, dammit, she had enjoyed herself with him. It was unexpected and neither had been on guard. In fact every barb they had tossed had had a foolish, funny point to it.

No, she didn't want him around. It was best that he was gone for the day. She wanted distance between them so that she could come to her senses.

"What's wrong with the transmitter?" she asked casually. "We're on the air, aren't we?"

"What's wrong with the transmitter?" Sara repeated, raising her eyes to the ceiling and contemplating the question. She was a tiny, plump woman with a pretty face and quick, intelligent eyes. Married, she had a year old daughter that her writer husband cared for during the long evenings when Sara worked. Inherited as an assistant when Julie was hired as moderator for *Night Talk*, they worked closely and harmoniously together.

"The station's on the air, but somewhere a gizmo is malfunctioning or something," Sara went on. "How's that for an explanation?"

"Pretty good." Julie waited a second or two, then said, "Has Casey Phillips been getting to you that much, Sara?"

"No, not really. I just hate to see you under pressure, that's all. Us lowly assistants can undoubtedly hold on to our jobs forever. It's only you big celebrities that have been taking the fallout." She stopped and looked curiously at Julie. "What's happened to you?" She smiled. "Ah, I was right. He's out of your hair and you suddenly look cool, calm and wonderfully rested.''

Julie laughed, but felt embarrassed by the sound. ''I suppose that's it.'' She wanted to talk about Casey, about their date the evening before, but she had no way of bringing the subject up. Sara had made her position on the matter of the station manager quite clear—as had Julie on a dozen occasions. How could she explain her sudden lapse the night before?

She couldn't, certainly not to herself, and not to Sara either.

''Well,'' she said, sighing deeply, ''let's get this show on the road.''

The afternoon went quickly but without incident, although every time the telephone rang, and it rang often, Julie's heart seemed to skip a beat. And each time she felt a faint disappointment that it wasn't Casey.

He didn't return to the station in time for her show. The faulty transmitter hadn't taken WRBZ off the air and Julie never did find out exactly what went wrong. She was, she realized, singularly uninterested in the mechanics of the thing. Her voice and brain were the instruments she took special care of. The rest she left to the experts.

In order to keep cranks off the air, all call-in programs were equipped with special seven-second devices, *Night Talk* included. Callers' voices were instantly recorded and played back over the air seven seconds later. This gave the engineer and Sara, who directed Julie's show from the booth, time to disconnect. Listeners weren't even aware of the time lapse.

About midway through her program that night, when Julie began taking her first calls, Casey's voice came on.

"What I want to know, Ms. Garrett, and you can ask this question of any member of your panel, is do you make the pesto sauce yourself or can it be purchased at any deli around town?"

She flushed, looking quickly at Sara in the control booth. Sara switched into the next call and the program went on smoothly after that. When the program was over, Sara came down into the studio.

"That crank call that came in around one o'clock? Pesto sauce? Was that some weird friend of yours? I'd have sworn it was Casey Phillips, except I know better."

Julie ducked her head, pretending to sift through some papers as if looking for something. Then she made up her mind. Sara would have to know something if Casey insisted on playing games. Then one of her guests interrupted her thoughts, inviting the group to the nearest bar.

Sara took up matters firmly. "I've ordered cabs for everybody," she said, giving Julie a wink. They made it a habit of sending their guests away at once and not seeing them after hours.

"Let's all pack it in," Julie said. She'd ride uptown with Sara, but by now she did not want to talk about Casey.

A simple question about Sara's baby took care of the conversation. When the cab stopped at the Ansonia, Julia had had her fill of stories of first teeth, first words and first attempts to walk. Saved, Julie thought, walking briskly into the building, by the baby.

The next day she was up and out of the apartment around noon, shopping for the makings of pesto genovese. She picked up fresh basil, some parsley, garlic, fresh olive oil, pignoli and Parmesan cheese.

She would put the sauce together in her blender and head out for her sister's house around four in the afternoon. She hadn't heard from Casey, and if he called, she was determined to be firm with him. He would not, repeat, *not* be invited to come along. Friday without him and his call when her program was on-air clinched it.

When she returned to her apartment, the telephone was ringing. She rushed in, counting the rings, dropping her package in the foyer. Yet for a long moment she didn't pick up the receiver. One more ring and the answering device would click in. It would be so easy to record the message. If it were Casey, she would know soon enough—*if* he was at the other end.

Then, somehow, the receiver was in her hand and she found herself putting it hesitantly to her ear. "Yes?"

"Two quarts of the stuff enough?"

"Two quarts? Good Lord, that should cost the entire defense budget." Her mind went blank. What was it she had planned to say to him?

"Perfect, because that's what I got. They suggested an extra bit of Parmesan. Half pound okay?"

"Oh, make it two pounds, Casey, as long as you're springing for it."

There was a faint pause. "Right. They said something about possibly taking along extra pignoli just in case."

"Oh absolutely, by the pound again. We'll try to make do." It was close to ten dollars a pound, she knew.

"You wouldn't be putting me on, Garrett?"

"Would I do that, Phillips?"

"No, Garrett, you wouldn't. You're entirely too serious and we'll have to do something about that. I'm renting a car. What time are we supposed to be there?"

She was quiet for a long moment. She could make the pesto sauce and be out of the apartment in an hour, take the 4:08 to Stamford and that would be the end of Casey Phillips.

"Hey, Garrett, you there?"

"Oh, why aren't you minding the station, Casey? Get out of my hair once and for all."

"It's Saturday. We rest, eat pesto alla genovese, make love."

"I don't know why I'm talking to you. Goodbye." Still she hesitated.

"Pick you up at three." He hung up. Leave it to Casey. He'd win, even in the matter of who hung up first.

"No," she said aloud to the buzz in the telephone receiver, "No you won't pick me up at three."

At three o'clock, she still hadn't made the pesto sauce. In fact, the fresh sprigs of basil sitting in a glass of water, showed the first signs of wilt. Oh well, she'd bring them along and use them for decoration or in the salad. The roots were still on them. Maybe her sister could plant them in the backyard or something.

When the doorman buzzed her from downstairs, there was nothing left to do. "Mr. Phillips says he's parked in a No Parking zone."

Good, let him get a ticket, she thought. "I'll be right down," she said in a mock-weary voice.

She wore a skirt of lilac-sprigged white cotton, a loose matching blouse over it and white sandals. There was a bathing suit in her capacious straw bag, and a present for her niece, Lindy. An evening's dinner and a swim in their pool, then back to the city, the visit for the spring season over. She didn't see her sister often. The six-year age difference had been an early deterrent to closeness; when they were both grown, geographical distance had been the other.

That and other things: her sister's bad first marriage; now her life in the suburbs, and Julie's obvious urban success. Their styles of living were incompatible. Both offered something that each of them wanted, she supposed.

Julie preferred not to go into it, for fear of discovering things both about herself and her sister that were better laid to rest.

Casey was waiting for her at the lobby door. He was wearing white jeans with a dark, open-necked shirt. Too handsome by far, she thought; a handsomeness one did not tire of—at least not yet.

"The car smells of one hundred percent garlic," he said at once. "Your sister may eat the pesto sauce, her family may eat the pesto sauce, her friends may eat the pesto sauce, but you, Julie Garrett, will not. That's an order."

She laughed. "Oh, but I adore it."

"Come on, Master Chef," he said, taking her arm and marching her out to the curb, "we'll drop the stuff off, take the requisite drink she'll undoubtedly offer us, and then go for dinner somewhere else. I left my family in California. I think all families should be a continent away, don't you?"

"You are the most absolutely take-charge man I've ever met, Casey," she said, and then obediently stepped into the car while he held the door for her. The vehicle was a small sports car containing what she supposed was a dangerous amount of horsepower. The scent of garlic and basil was very faint and quite pleasant.

"You're such a liar," she said, when he put the car into gear.

"About what? I'm an extremely up-front person."

"About the garlic. Never mind."

"You wait until you get a cleaning bill that states 'Garlic smell impossible to remove from dimity dress.' That *is* what they call that, isn't it?" he asked, referring to what she was wearing.

"More or less."

"Whatever it is, I like you in it. Do you realize that all I've ever seen you in is a modified career girl uniform?"

"I'm a career girl, Casey. I've an extensive wardrobe of 'pert, neat little costumes' as they would say in the fashion magazines. You know, the kind that go from business to cocktails, with the removal or addition of a little jacket? Etcetera, etcetera."

He cast her a quick smile. "Running that radio show of yours hasn't left you bereft of words, has it?"

She gave him a smile in return. She had no idea at what point she had thrown in the towel and decided to go with him, but she wasn't sorry. So far. "No. Too bad Sara cut you off last night. I'd have liked to say a few words to you over fifty thousand kilowatts."

He blew his horn and cursed a cabdriver. She settled back in her seat. It was going to be one interesting day, she thought.

The house her sister lived in with her daughter and lawyer husband was a large rambling Colonial standing on two acres of valuable land, with a stream running along the back. Leafy maples at least a hundred years old dominated the front lawn, which was velvety smooth, and freshly mown. Set down with artless symmetry were azaleas in full flower and rhododendrons in all shades of pink and purple.

"That's it," Julie said, feeling an unexpected pride in the beauty of the place, as though the elegance it breathed would cling to her as well. The driveway was already packed with cars. Julie expected it. It seemed that Bobbie always asked a mob when she invited Julie up.

"Nice," Casey said with admiration. He moved up the street and found a parking space. "That's what I like about the Northeast. Comfortable old houses surrounded by the leafy green of venerable old trees."

"What about sequoias?" she asked.

"Too old, too venerable. Only California could make them up. Give me a tree you can hug." He helped her out of the car and handed her the shopping bag of sauce. "Might as well tell your sister you made it."

"I'll tell her no such thing." She handed back the bag and hurried down the street. "Come on, they're all out back."

She found her sister in a crowd of people wearing all manner of dress. She was standing apart, surveying the scene, a tall, lanky woman with a tiny nose, wide mouth, and glittering dark-brown eyes. Her hair, which was black and worn shoulder length, carried the first signs of gray in it. Too young for gray, Julie thought, giving her sister a hug.

"Bobby, this is Casey Phillips," she said quickly. "Casey, my sister." She turned and saw her brother-in-law, big, blond and good-looking, ambling toward them, a drink in his hand.

"Little sister, how are you doing?" he asked in the familiar tone he always adopted with her. He planted a kiss on her cheek.

"Dan Blackman, this is Casey Phillips," she said, as the two men shook hands.

"Glad you could come," Dan said. "Can I get you a drink?"

"Where's Lindy?" she asked, referring to her niece. Her sister gave her an anxious look.

"Oh, she'll be down in a few minutes."

"I brought a little something for her," Julie said. "And here," she added, appropriating the package Casey was carrying, "is your pesto sauce, a gift from Casey. I didn't make it, but it comes from the best shop in New York."

Her sister looked inside the package and laughed. "Enough for an army, *and* the navy, come to think of it. I don't believe this."

"You'd better," Julie said. She caught Casey glaring at her, eyebrow raised.

Her sister, tucking an arm through hers, drew her to the striped tent that covered part of the lawn and was set up for cocktails. A dozen feet from the tent was the swimming pool, where noisy youngsters were already playing. "Who's the gorgeous hunk?"

"Somebody I work with at the station. I forgot to tell him to bring a bathing suit."

"Dan has a spare." Bobbie paused and nodded in their direction. "Anything . . . you know?"

Julie leaned over and, laughing, spontaneously kissed her sister on the cheek. "No, Bobbie, no *anything*."

She was standing at the pool five minutes later, contemplating the youngsters playing there and wondering what had happened to her niece, when Casey came up behind her. "Let's go," he said. "I've had my drink, you've had your drink. The amenities are over with. From the look on your brother-in-law's face, and your sister's, they won't even know whether you're here or gone. What the devil are these events for, anyway?"

"How do I know," she said, turning angrily on him. "Spring solstice, for all I know. It's a warm, glorious day. I'm thinking of taking a swim."

He grinned. "Wonderful. I'd like to see you in a bathing suit."

"You always have the last word, don't you? Here," she said, handing him her untouched drink. "Hold this. I'm going upstairs to see my niece."

"Then we'll leave," he said. He tasted her drink. "What the devil is this concoction?"

"Ginger ale with mint."

She left him standing there and made her way across the lawn. She went quickly up the stairs to the enclosed back porch. There she found her sister engrossed in conversation with an elderly couple. Bobbie stood facing the lawn below, however, her eye almost certainly on her husband. Julie didn't disturb them but went on into the house, through the kitchen where a cook and helper were bending over plates of hors d'oeuvres.

Her contribution of the pesto sauce was certainly not needed, she realized, wondering if it were Bobbie's way of making certain she would come.

Julie had come but both she and Casey had been left to their own devices. Sisters. As she climbed the stairs to her niece's room, she thought with some amusement that it might make an interesting program.

A gentle knock on the teenager's door got no response. "Lindy? Are you there?" She knocked again. "It's Aunt Julie."

She could hear rustling and then Lindy suddenly shrieked with pleasure. "Aunt Julie?" The door was pulled open and Lindy fell on her. "Mom didn't tell me you were coming to her stupid party."

"Well, I'm here," she said, embracing her niece, "so you can come out of hiding now."

Lindy gave her a sharp look and then lowered her lashes. She was tall for her age, just shy of sixteen, with Julie's light hair and her mother's dark eyes. "Mom tell you I was hiding?"

"No, but I expected you to be down there. I brought my famous spaghetti sauce, only I didn't make it this time. And I've got someone with me."

Lindy took her arm and drew her into the room. It was large and feminine with pink roses on the wallpaper, and white ruffled window curtains. The room was triumphantly ruined with too many huge posters of rock stars and tons of plush animals, and looked as if a war between Lindy and her mother had broken out over who the girl was, and what she might become. She dragged Julie over to the window that looked out on the garden. "Which one is he? Is he a movie star? What's his name?"

"He's over there, the light-haired one talking to your father."

"That's not my father." Lindy turned away without commenting on Casey, as though she had lost all interest in the subject.

Julie suspected she was trespassing where she wasn't wanted. She reached into her bag. "I brought something for you."

Lindy tore open the paper, and found a cassette inside. "Hey, neat," she said, waving it in the air. "A Bruce Springsteen tape. Yay, I don't even have this one."

"Okay, come on downstairs," Julie said.

"Aunt Julie, I don't want to go down there," Lindy said through gritted teeth, her face flushing.

It was the stubbornness Bobbie always attributed to her first husband, something Lindy seemed to have been born with. Today, Julie thought wearily, she had had quite enough of it. Whatever teenage nonsense was involved, it was between Lindy and her parents. "I'll see you later, then," she said quietly.

As she was about to close the door behind her, Lindy called out in a soft, apologetic voice, "Aunt Julie?"

Julie turned, poked her head in the door. "Yes?"

Her niece's face was still pink, but she shook her head. "No," she said, "nothing."

Casey was waiting for her on the porch. Bobbie had gone back out onto the crowded lawn. "Let's go," he said. "I've already made our excuses."

"You what?" She had the funny feeling of being manipulated by just about everyone: her sister, Lindy, even Dan.

"Julie," he said, taking her shoulders between strong fingers, "we're leaving with your sister's blessing. I said we had this crashing bore of a meeting we had to go to in Greenwich."

"Well, that's ridiculous." She ran out onto the lawn and found her sister engaged in what she was certain was a low, tense conversation with her husband. "Bobbie," she said, planting herself between them, "I'm sorry we have to leave. It's just one of those stupid things." The words had come from nowhere, but saying them gave her a sudden, inexplicable feeling of relief.

Her sister looked at her. "What? Right. Casey told me. Call me, would you?"

Kisses were exchanged. "Let's go," she said, when she found Casey coming up behind her.

She sat in the car and let the taped music lull her senses. She was back in Brookline, Massachusetts, her sister always so grown-up, then gone when Julie was barely in her teens. Brookline. She didn't remember her father. He had left when she was two years old, and died in California when she was twelve. Her mother had supported them at first by waitressing, but after a while she became housekeeper for the most affluent family in town. Julie had grown up looking at wealth. The large kitchen her mother ruled over had been her first classroom.

The lesson she had learned was that money made life easy, and that the lack of it relegated one to the back door.

She realized later why Bobbie had left, why she had made an unfortunate marriage. She had learned the lesson, too, and how differently the sisters had gone about changing their lives.

Julie had caught on early that education, coupled with hard work, would take her far away from Brookline and the back door. There was college on a scholarship, work wherever she could get it—waitress, typist, baby-sitter—she'd been them all. One summer she had cleaned houses, spending all her spare time and cash buying old fur coats. During the fall semester she sold the mended, secondhand coats to students, convincing them it was the latest rage. She smiled, recalling the old raccoons and minks, that had chased each other on slim, girlish figures across the campus.

And Bobbie, six years older than she, had trapped herself in a bad first marriage. After her divorce, when Lindy was ten years old, she had supported herself by running a nursery school in Connecticut. Dan was her lawyer, and when they married, following his divorce, he set her up in style.

Contrasts in solutions to the same problem.

Four

———

Why the heavy silence?'' Casey remarked when they were well away from her sister's house and on the road going north.

"Oh, I don't know," Julie said. "There's just something that depresses me about that house." She stopped, wondering why she was opening up to Casey when she had never even admitted it to herself before. "The size, the big trees, all those rooms; I'm not certain what. Could be I'm too used to efficiency apartments by now."

"It's not the house; it's the people in it, Julie."

"The people in it?" She turned toward him angrily. "How can you say that? Bobbie's my sister, and I love her daughter."

"Bobbie's your sister and you love her daughter. Interesting phraseology, that."

"You know what I mean, Casey."

He nodded. "Sure I do. You love your sister." Then he added, "But Dan is another story."

Casey cast a sidelong glance at her. "His hands were shaking and I think he had one too many."

"He has a lot of pressure in his job."

"Well, don't we all?" He lifted his hand from the wheel and splayed his fingers out. "No signs of shaking; none at all."

"Casey," she said tiredly, "knock it off. My brother-in-law's been in line for a partnership in his law firm, and now it looks as if he might be passed over. Meanwhile, they've been living high on the hog in anticipation of things getting better. He's feeling the pressure."

"It's more than what *he* feels, I'm afraid. That tension pervades the whole atmosphere."

"He saved my sister's life," she told him quietly.

"Then I hate to think of what the alternative was."

"Oh, I don't want to talk about him anymore," Julie said, irritated that Casey had picked up on something she hadn't wanted to face. She wondered just how much Bobbie knew, and then remembered catching her sister on the porch, looking down over the lawn to where Dan stood. Her sister was no fool.

"I agree. We've talked about them long enough," Casey said. They drove for a while, both silent as if they needed to rid themselves of the lingering feeling of unpleasantness.

After a while Casey spoke up. "I've just the thing to make up for dragging you out of what promised to be the party of the year."

"Sarcasm not appreciated," she threw in tiredly.

"What we're going to do," he said, as though he hadn't heard her, "is head for the coziest inn this side of the Mississippi. Real old-world charm, and a lake that will take your breath away."

She looked at him, surprised. "How do you know so much about Connecticut? I wouldn't think it was required reading in your geography class back in Beverly Hills."

"Oh, I'm a well-traveled chap. Anyway, I know the people who own the place. Transplanted Californians who came East a couple of years ago. Never thought they'd stay, but they wanted to become innkeepers. Christmas in Connecticut and all that. The place was a success from the start."

"What's the name?"

"Lakeview," he said with a grin. "The Lakeview Inn. Clever. I haven't made it back, unfortunately, since the last time I was in New York a couple of years ago, but it's charming."

"Nice to know you appreciate something about the East," Julie remarked. She was on the defensive and nervous and was afraid to face the reason why.

"There's a lot about the East I appreciate. You, for instance."

Julie looked away, flustered by his comment, while he took a sharp turn to the right down a narrow country road.

"We're almost there," he said.

"Are you sure it's this way?" Huge leafy trees made a bower of the road, closing it in.

"Trust me, Julie."

"Where have I heard that before?"

Suddenly there it was, a beautiful old Colonial house, barely seen through the trees. The setting sun, its rays splintered through the leafy canopy, cast a golden hue on the scene, and then disappeared, leaving lavender shadows in its place.

Casey pulled the car into a circular driveway, a puzzled look on his face. There were no other cars and no lights in the windows of the inn.

"Casey, there's no one here," Julie said, feeling the silence of the place all around her. "Are you sure this is it?"

"Lakeview Inn," Casey said. "There's the sign." He opened the car door and sprinted toward the front entrance.

When Julie came up behind him, he was trying to peer without success through closed, curtained windows. Then he turned to a small notice pinned to the front door. "That's the explanation."

Julie stepped in front of him and read the notice out loud. "Closed for renovations."

"So much for surprises," he said, grasping her arms and resting his chin on her head.

"I thought you never made mistakes. I thought you called the shots and never got anything wrong." She moved out from under his touch and faced him, laughing. It was good to see his embarrassment. It made him human.

"Okay, I deserve that," he told her. "Anyway, let's not let the visit go to waste. I'll show you the lake and then we can get going. I know a great burger joint." He took her arm and led her around the porch and out back.

"I know a great place where they're serving pesto sauce," she said. "Why the devil didn't you call your friends beforehand?"

"Julie, believe me, they never close, not for Christmas, not for Fourth of July, not even for Arbor Day. Especially not for Arbor Day. This way to the lake." He took her single file down an overgrown path behind the house.

"Are you sure it's still there? It could be a housing development by now," Julie said.

"No one would be that sacrilegious. It would be against nature to fill in the lake."

"When was the last time you looked at real estate prices in this area?"

He reached for her hand and stepped through a grove of trees to behold a small, silvery lake surrounded by trees. A solitary swan floated lazily by, ruffling its feathers. The air was still, broken only by the cries of an unseen bird. On the far side of the lake was a lone house with a yellow light in its window.

Casey, behind her, pulled her back so that his body supported her. They stood quietly at the water's edge, Julie leaning into him. She could feel his breath against her hair and realized she could almost forget that it was wrong, as it had been all day, for them to be alone together. Almost was the operative word.

"I know another place," he said softly after a while.

"You only get one chance," Julie said. "I think it's time to head back to New York."

"I promised you dinner."

"I'll take a rain check."

"Will you now?" He held her tightly and pulled her around. She knew it would happen in that instant when she looked up into his eyes. Slivers of blue gazed at her with just a hint of amusement in them. His mouth came down hard on hers as she rocked in his arms.

"I don't think—" she began, trying to break free of his grasp.

"That's right, don't think. It's better that way." With his lips just above hers, he whispered, "You don't know what you do to me, Julie."

"And you'll be only too happy to show me," she said, pulling away.

He reached for her but she stepped aside, all too aware of the rush of desire that had flared up at his touch. "Don't be afraid, Julie."

"Not now, maybe not ever, but certainly not now," she said, facing him defiantly.

He put up his hands in mock surrender and she walked quickly back along the dark, tangled path to the car, aware of him following her.

She opened the car door and slipped into the safety of the interior, holding her breath as Casey slid into the driver's seat. He put the key into the ignition and turned it.

"Damn," he said under his breath as the engine refused to catch. He slammed his hands against the steering wheel and tried the ignition once again. There wasn't even a click.

"I don't believe it," Julie said. "You wouldn't pull a trick as old as that. The gas gauge certainly doesn't read empty."

"Engine's flooded, maybe," he told her, but she could hear the doubt in his voice. "We could wait a few minutes."

"I don't suppose we have a choice."

She leaned back and glanced at her watch. They didn't speak during the few minutes Casey let pass before trying again.

"Probably out of gas." He got out of the car and spent some time peering under the hood with a flashlight. Then he slammed down the hood, came back and looked through the window.

"There isn't a house or a gas station for miles," Julie said. "You wouldn't happen to have a spare can of gasoline or something in the trunk that you'll conveniently find later?"

"I suppose it would be futile to explain that this wasn't planned."

"Strange as it may seem to you, Casey, I do believe you." Julie couldn't resist smiling. "No one with an ounce of self-respect would pull that old chestnut out of the fire— even you."

"Thanks for small compliments." He came around to her side, opened the door and handed her out. "Come on, there's only one choice."

"And that is?" For a moment they stood very close, her hand still clasped in his.

"We're going to break and enter. They must have a phone someplace."

"Odd they don't live here."

"Maybe they're off renovating themselves." He began to go slowly around the old building, trying windows. He found one at the back that gave easily. Casey lifted himself over the sill in one swift movement. "I'll get the front door."

Dusk had settled in and eerie shadows cavorted along the grounds as Julie went back to the front porch. Casey opened the massive double door and let her in with a sweeping bow. "Excuse the clutter. It must be the maid's day off. Let's see now, there must be a light switch along the wall here. Ah, here we go."

There was a click and a bare overhead bulb lit up, swinging crazily on its wire. They stood in a large, airy foyer filled with furniture under tarpaulins, and buckets of paint. The air smelled of oil and turpentine and damp wood rot.

"Well, it ain't much," Casey commented, "but it's home."

"What we want is a telephone," Julie reminded him.

"Right. We can register later. You start in the living room, and I'll look in the kitchen."

She was tentatively lifting paint-splattered sheets when Casey called. "I've found it, Julie. In the kitchen."

By the time she came in, however, he was waving the receiver at her. "Disconnected. I guess they figured the painter would call home if he had the chance, home no doubt being Hawaii." He pulled up a stool for her. "Have a seat while we figure out our options."

Julie shook her head, but sat down nevertheless. The kitchen was a huge affair of chrome and steel, with very little Colonial flavor. "There's not a soul in the entire world who would believe this, Casey."

"Let's not tell anyone."

"You're not kidding. This is one little adventure I'm going to play close to the chest."

He came over to her and took up her hand. "The modus operandi is as follows. I'll try to scout up something to eat. You, on the other hand, will take a tour of the place. See what shape the bedrooms are in."

"What?" She realized she had begun to shout. "See what shape the bedrooms are in? Now why would I want to do that?"

"Just a suggestion," he said, giving her a crooked smile.

She pulled her hand from his grasp, aware of her childish reaction, but something told her that if she didn't get away from him, and soon, she could easily succumb. She got down off the stool, allowing time to forestall any objections his or her heart might make. "No way, Mr. Phillips. Do you realize you've been trying to run my life from the moment we met? At the station, and even at my sister's house, and now this. There's civilization around here somewhere and I'm going to find it. Across the lake." She went over to the kitchen window and drew the curtains aside. "Over there, a light. It couldn't be more than..."

"A mile away," he finished for her. "If you trace the edge of the lake. If you try the highway, five miles as the crow doesn't fly."

"I'm getting out of here," she told him, "even if I have to walk all the way back to New York." She marched past him out of the kitchen and went storming to the front door.

It was pitch-black with a silence punctuated only by the deep-bellied call of a bullfrog on the lakefront. She had strayed off the driveway when she tried to take a shortcut away from Casey and his amused smile. Now tripping as her heels dug into the carpet of leaves underfoot, she had no idea where the road was. Glancing back toward the house through thick branches like huge hands that seemed to grab at her, she could see the only beacon of light in the dark of the night.

Straight ahead, it had to be straight ahead. Branches clawed at her, and something fluttered in her face and wheeled away. She stifled a scream. How could this have happened? she asked herself. The fear that crept along her skin was totally different from any she had ever felt on lonely city streets where anything could happen. Yet she had to chance it. Any fool with half a mind could tell what would have happened if she had not run away. Casey, exuding charm and the kind of sex appeal she felt helpless against, needed only to smile and lead her to bed. She, fool that she was, would have gone willingly along.

He was laughing now; she was certain of it. He hadn't followed her or called her back. He expected her to take a dozen steps into the darkness and then to turn around, frightened and crying. Never.

There was a low growl from somewhere on her left, and then a furry thing wrapped itself around her leg. She held her breath, cursing her stupidity. Getting herself killed trying to run away from Casey was not exactly how she planned to end her day, either.... This time she gave in to the scream and turning back to the inn, stumbled once more through the brush.

When she saw Casey he was leaning against the porch post with his arms folded across his chest. He didn't move as she came running thankfully toward him. Then the heel of her shoe gave way and she tripped, wrenching her ankle.

"Julie." He took the steps two at a time, and when he got close, Julie threw herself into his arms.

"Something horribly furry," she said, struggling to catch her breath, "sort of crawled along my leg. It scared the hell out of me." Her ankle began to throb.

"Okay, it's all okay now," he said, cradling her in his arms. "A cat, that's all."

"An attack cat, then."

"Come on, consider yourself rescued. I found the fixings for tuna and crackers and instant coffee. After that you can go to sleep in one of the upstairs bedrooms. We'll get the whole thing straightened out tomorrow," he said in a serious, practical way. She flushed as she buried her head on his chest. He knew exactly why she had run away and he was telling her that he would put it aside, for now, anyway.

She felt a searing pain in her foot as she pressed down on it. "Casey, I'm afraid I hurt my ankle just now."

Without a word he swooped her up in his arms. She gratefully cuddled against him, not caring any more.

"They've completed two bedrooms, torn apart six or seven, and left a neat four or five untouched," Casey said.

"I've selected the *Moby Dick* suite for you, although there isn't a nautical idea in sight."

"Not one of the refurbished ones, I hope. I'd feel a little pushy taking over one of those." He still held her in his arms. He smelled good and felt good, but Julie knew that the sooner she got away from him, the better it would be all around.

"I just figured you'd look fantastic in roses." The door was open and he brought her in and sat her down on the edge of the bed. The room was lit by a lamp which cast a soft, pale glow. She was aware of rose-patterned wallpaper and a canopied bed with the same pattern on it, but the problem for the time being was her foot.

"Let's see it," he said, bending down. "This hurt?" He touched the tender spot.

She winced. "Like hell."

"Okay, what we have here is a hurt ankle."

"Thank you, Dr. Phillips."

"Prescription, a good hot soaking. By the oddest chance, I tiptoed into the basement not fifteen minutes ago and turned on the hot water heater."

"You must know your friends very well," she said.

He gave her a satisfied smile. "I'll send them a check. For now, I'll run a bath for you complete with bubbles. Then we'll have our repast and off to dreamland for you, my girl."

"Are you sure you're just talking about a hot bath?" Julie asked.

"Trust me," Casey said, still fingering her ankle.

"I did. Look where it got me."

She turned her ankle slowly, bearing with the pain, sensing that it would be worse if she babied herself. "I'll take care of everything myself," she said. "Tripping like that was really playing right into your—" She stopped, laughed, and finished the sentence. *"Hands."* She lay down on the bedspread and gazed up at him.

"I'm pooped. Casey," she said, yawning, "you've been trouble from the very first day you stepped into my life."

He reached down and briefly touched his hand to her forehead. "Have I now? It's not quite how I view it."

"Of course," she said sleepily, her eyes closing of their own accord.

"Do you always get what you want?" She asked the question, not quite certain if it was precisely the one she really wanted to ask. He didn't answer and she yawned once again before slipping easily into sleep.

When Casey tapped her gently awake she had no idea how much time had gone by, nor even for a moment where she was.

"Hot bath ready, madame. Towel and back scrubber ready, too." He reached for her but she brushed him away.

"I can take care of myself," she said, as she put her foot gingerly on the floor. There was a slight pain, soon gone when she stood up and tested her ankle. "Good as new. Now if you'll excuse me, sir."

When she stepped into the tub, which as promised was filled with bubbles, it was with a grateful sigh. He was right, she thought, stretching out in the hot water. It was just what was needed—for her foot, her temper, and her view of the night that lay ahead. She closed her eyes and drifted off into a daydream. In it, Casey was reaching for her, a knowing smile on his face. Julie was once more struck by his sexuality, made all the more menacing because she didn't want him to stop. She opened her eyes quickly, sensing the danger that lay in the daydream.

Later, toweling herself dry, she heard sounds coming from the bedroom.

"Casey?"

"Need any help?"

"No, thank you, just wondering why you're still around." He should not be there, she told herself, reflecting on the promise he had made earlier. *We'll discuss it all in the morning.* She slipped on the flannel robe she found hanging on the door, determined to deal with him at once. The robe was miles too big with sleeves that hung down past the tips of her fingers. Luckily it came with a belt, which she tied tightly around her waist. As she opened the bathroom door, she could hear the crackling of a fire in the fireplace.

Casey was bending over the fire, pushing at a log with a pair of tongs. There was a tray of food on a table nearby. Somehow he had managed to scout up a silver coffee urn.

"Oh, Casey," she said against her will, allowing pleasure to seep into her voice.

He turned and she could hear him quickly catch his breath. He caught her eyes and held them for an instant, as if she had somehow tricked him.

"Thanks for the fire," she said, going over to it and spreading her hands to take the warmth. It was going to be difficult.

"How's the foot?"

"In working order." She went back to the bed and perched on the edge.

He came over to her. "You've a bruise on your neck, too. Lie back."

"Casey, I'm all right," she said, resisting the pressure of his hand on her shoulder.

"Liniment. Found it along with a lot of other medical supplies in the laundry room when I was in the basement. How can I rub it on your ankle if you don't cooperate?"

"I don't need my ankle rubbed with liniment or anything else." Nevertheless she pulled herself up on the bed and settled back against the pillow. "There's a faint, nearly nonexistent twinge. That's all, Casey. You're making too big a thing of it."

"Sure I am." He pulled the robe from across her ankle and a moment later, Julie felt the touch of his fingertips against her skin. The liniment was cool at first, but the warmth built up steadily as his fingers massaged it into her skin.

"You must have had some fight with that furry monster," he said. "You've a couple of scratches that could use a little antibiotic."

"Dr. Phillips, you've done quite enough," she said, waving her hand toward the crackling fire and tray of food.

"That's that," he said, patting her ankle. "We'll get to the scratches in a minute."

"Casey," she said in a warning voice. He had taken his tie off and his shirt was open at the collar. His tanned, smoothly muscled torso seemed to block everything else from her vision. Julie was dimly aware that she was holding herself in check. This man was reaching some part of her being that hadn't been touched before, and she shivered with a combination of fear and anticipation.

"Casey," she said, hearing the tension in her voice, "All I want is a good night's sleep before we tackle the problem of getting out of here."

"You win." He raised his hands once again in mock surrender. He went over to the food tray and returned with a glass of brandy for her. "Drink this. Compliments of the house."

She took a sip. The warm liquid went down smoothly. She handed him the remains of the drink. He sat down next to her and raised the glass in a salute before finishing off its contents.

"Not a bad ending to the day, is it, Julie?" He reached out and slipped his fingers through her hair before pressing her gently back against the pillows.

"Casey," she began and then stopped. His hand rested for a moment on her neck and when he reached for the collar of her robe and tugged lightly at it, she knew she was powerless to stop him. "What was in that brandy?" she murmured.

With a slow, deliberate gesture he pushed the robe from her shoulders to reveal her naked breasts. His look was a caress, as if he had waited a long time for the moment and wouldn't be hurried.

He bent over her. "Don't put me off, Julie. Don't make me wait." She could feel the warmth of his breath against her lips. "You don't know how much I want you. From the very beginning when I first heard your voice, I felt it then, a warm, seductive sound, a sultry quality that reached out and pinned me to the wall. It got me." He pressed his lips against hers for a long moment. "Then I saw you and what I felt overwhelmed me. For the first time in my life, all the pieces seemed to fit. It was as if some ancient siren's call had ensnared me."

"I don't believe a word you're saying," she answered, feeling the sensation of his words as though they had shape and substance, "but you can keep on saying it." She wound her arms around his neck, knowing that she wouldn't, couldn't stop what was happening. "Casey," she began, but he cut off her next words by filling her mouth with his thrusting, searching tongue, as if he had been starving for the taste of her.

He raised his head and gazed longingly at her as he ran his hand down her body. Impatiently, he thrust the robe aside and spread it about her. Julie moved to her side and curled up a bit at his frank appraisal, but he touched her chin, turning her face toward him. "It's me, Julie," he said softly. "Don't hide."

"It's too fast, Casey. You're not giving me time to breathe." But she wondered whether he was even listening to her.

"I knew what you would look like," he said in a tight whisper. He reached out and cupped her breast and after another moment he moaned softly. His head dipped lower and his tongue found the sensitive peak.

She knew then with a kind of awesome finality that she wanted him to make love to her. She had known it when she ran out into the night, hoping to escape her own desire, and knew it now as his hands touched her with long, hypnotic strokes.

Her body rose to meet him, arching away from the bed. A languid warmth spread through her, even as a faint, nagging worry struggled to hold on to part of her brain. She should stop now, before she crossed the line to where there would be no returning. His lips found her mouth, and then as though hungry to know every part of her, traced feathery kisses along her face.

Julie drew her fingers through his hair, pulling him closer, all thoughts of sending him away gone forever.

Then he stopped for a moment, as though he, too, had second thoughts, while the fire sent glittering points of light into his eyes. He shrugged off whatever doubts had assailed him, as he silently, powerfully trapped her beneath the weight of his body. His arms wrapped around her, blocking any attempt at retreat.

A wondrous feeling rippled through her as nerve endings that were new to her pulsed wildly at his touch. With a growl of impatience, he undid the belt and pulled off her robe, his mouth assaulting her lips, his tongue thrust against her teeth. All trace of anything but the wild emotions that soared through her body was gone. Her skin felt hot with an exquisite ache of longing as his hands explored her body. It was as if he were impatient to know every inch of her.

His mouth was hot and wet as he closed it over one rose-crested peak. He tugged at her gently, and then she felt the exquisite torture as he flicked his tongue lightly over the sensitive flesh. His hand was at the small of her back, urging her forward, pressing her against his hard, ready body. She moaned softly as the scent of him filled her and sent her blood pounding in her veins. She felt helpless, as if she were drowning in a whirling vortex that had no bottom. He was still for a moment and she opened her eyes to find him looking at her with a devouring gaze that shot through her with the sharpness of a bullet.

At last, with a soft moan of protest, he rose and stripped off his clothes. Julie watched him, unashamed, knowing that she wanted to see him. He looked down at her with hungry passion before he descended again.

His weight pinned her to the mattress, his body lean, muscular, hard with an athlete's prowess. His naked chest pressed against her breasts as he shifted his legs and with his knee parted her thighs. She returned his kiss with a hunger that matched his, knowing she wanted him to go slowly and yet needing him to hurry. She knew she was wildly out of control, trembling, clawing at him in a frenzy she didn't understand.

When she spoke, her words came sharply, wanting him to know that this was new to her. "I never—" but they were broken off when he whispered gently into her mouth.

"I know."

His lips trailed down her throat as he slid down her body, stopping only when he came to the juncture of her thighs. She cried his name in joy and panic when she felt his lips touch the sensitive flesh. She held her breath as he kissed her more intimately and with an artistry that left her completely in his power. A shudder rippled through her as he raised himself until he was poised over her, and claimed her lips once again.

His eyes locked with hers as he moved to enter her. He was slow at first, and then he pressed deeply, thrusting hard until she felt all of him. She cried out, clinging to him. When he began to move, he still watched her as if he were cataloging her pleasure, memorizing her rapture.

"Oh, if only you knew how good you felt," he said as his mouth found her breast once again.

"Tell me," she whispered, moving with him.

"There are no words." Then with a passion Julie had never known before, he drove into her, carrying her along with him on a long, seemingly endless wave of ecstasy.

The room was dark with only the faintest glow of red embers in the fireplace. Casey's breathing was deep and even. Julie could feel it on her naked chest as she held him close. That was it, she thought with a soft sigh, that what she had been waiting for, and she hadn't even known she was waiting. She would think about the rest of it later, when her head was clear, when it didn't matter anymore. Time would tell if what she felt for Casey Phillips was love. Right now, it felt like it, with not a worry in sight.

He awoke once more in the night and reached for her. Without words they made love again, slowly this time, savoring every moment, knowing it was precious and special. When Julie fell asleep once more, it was with a sense of peace and fulfillment that she had thought impossible to attain.

Casey was sitting up in bed when she came out of the bath in the morning. She had found a large pink bath towel and wrapped it around herself.

"Finally up, I see." She came back to the bed and climbed in next to him, smiling, believing her smile could easily turn into a purr.

He grinned back and reached for her. "Out of that towel, Garrett. I want to see what you look like in the morning."

"Forget it," she said. "I'm at my best in the firelight." She cuddled against him as he pulled the blanket around them both.

"You smell good, Garrett. You taste good, you feel good and you look good." He began gently to rub her back. "I've been thinking."

"Oh, have you now? That doesn't sound like the Casey I know."

"I do all my best thinking in the morning." He pulled the blanket away and then the towel. Tracing his fingers along her body, as if he had total possession of her, he said, "I've been thinking, and the conclusion I've drawn is—"

"Casey," she interrupted, "this had better be good." She waited, holding her breath while his eyes took in her nude body.

"Just that you should be seen as well as heard. You have brains, beauty and a body, not necessarily in that order. It's a great package. The way I see it," he went on with increasing enthusiasm, "we should think big. In other words, telly, as the English would say. Radio is wasting one beautiful half of you, love."

"Casey," she began but then held back the irritation that was creeping up on her. This was the man in whose arms she had slept, and she was no longer anxious to do battle with him. "I'm happy with my program," she finished lamely.

"Peanuts," he said. "I'm talking about the big time. You don't know what you've got. Use it. You should be on the fast track. You've got a quirky kind of sex appeal that should make you a front-runner."

"You're not listening to me," she said patiently. "I don't want to use my sex appeal, quirky or otherwise. I want to use me."

"You're a natural, Julie." He bent over and kissed her lips and for a moment she wanted to tear away from him. She hated what he was saying but he felt so good, she knew she couldn't bear being away from him. "Look," he said, his expression quite serious, "get rid of your agent. I know somebody better. With your body and that face you should be on television."

"Casey, I'll handle my own career. I've done quite well so far. I don't think the way you do, obviously."

"I know what I'm talking about." He stopped and then reached out and brushed his fingers quickly through her hair. "You used it on me and I didn't even know what hit me."

"What?" She moved away, suddenly feeling that she had lost something, although if pressed, she couldn't have said what.

"Come on, Julie. You're not a novice at this game. You know what I mean. There's that mixture of innocence and age-old sensuality about you that just reaches out and grabs."

"Casey," she said carefully, "if I told you that you're making me angry, would you stop?"

"Stop what?"

"Stop what you're saying. Stop trying to run my life. And last but not least, stop insulting me."

His expression was one of hurt innocence. "How am I insulting you?"

"If you don't know..." She took in a deep sigh. "I didn't play tricks on you; I'm just me, as you see me."

He leaned back against the headboard and crossed his arms over his chest, grinning. "Well, neither one of us was born yesterday, Julie. I'm just telling you to use what you've got to your advantage."

"I see," she said coldly. "And you're just the one who can see to it that I wiggle in the right places." She felt drained and suddenly didn't want his touch any longer.

"You've got the picture," he told her softly with something like triumph in his voice.

"Oh, Casey, I've got the picture all right."

Just then a horn sounded outside and the gears of a truck could be heard.

She got quickly out of bed and went over to the window. "I believe the workmen have arrived. Wonderful." She picked up her clothes and went over to the bathroom door. "We seem to have come to a parting of the ways in this discussion. I'm going to get dressed. Then I'm going to go downstairs and use my famous technique to get someone to drive me to the station, wherever that is. I'll leave you to explain all this." She waved her hand around the room. "I'm sure you'll manage all right."

"Julie."

She closed the door harder than she had intended and then stood there for a long, silent moment.

Five

───

It was Monday morning. Julie had spent what was left of
Sunday with an old college friend who had unexpectedly
come to town and rescued her from concentrating on what
had happened with Casey Phillips. Still, in spite of a mu-
seum visit, pleasant talk and a late dinner, Julie slept fit-
fully that night, tossing in and out of unfinished dreams of
Casey Phillips.

At last she gave in and got up for good at eight. She
counted four hours of broken sleep, took a shower, and
was sitting up in bed with a cup of coffee and toast pretending to read when the telephone rang.

"Julie?" She recognized the high-pitched, nasal accent
of the station's telephone operator.

"This is she. Kitty?" She answered cautiously with a
kind of foreboding that the day, which was already out of
kilter, would get worse.

"Emergency, emergency," the operator said with a laugh. "You know Opie Hart? He was just on the phone screaming to get hold of you. I said I'd have you call."

Trouble, Julie thought with something amounting to hope. It struck her that she really wanted a mad, mad day in which nothing went exactly right until the moment the show went on the air. Then, with consummate control she would host a program that would have her on the cover of *Time* the following week.

"What's his number?" she asked. "He didn't happen to say what it's about?"

"Something about Merv Griffin being in town and . . ."

"Say no more," said Julie. She took Opie's number and dialed him immediately.

The designer wasn't at his showroom, but she tracked him down at the studio where he was making a telecast with Merv Griffin.

"Opie," she said at once, "that's wonderful. You can plug your Merv Griffin appearance on *Night Talk*. Kill two birds with one stone."

"Darling, that's what I'm calling about," he said in the suave, continental, faintly babying tone he affected. "It's an absolute drag, but I'm off to Paris right after this. Honestly, you can't cut yourself into little pieces; I'll end up in sixty places all at once. You'll have to excuse me, pet. It's a certifiable wonder I was able to find the time to call you. I can't even remember my own name these days. Forgive, forgive, forgive, yes, pet?"

She smiled. Ordinarily she would have found herself easing into hysteria, but Opie's bowing out just like that firmed her determination. Get Casey Phillips the best way she knew how—through *Night Talk*. Somehow, some way, starting at once.

"Of course, Opie. I always have a standby waiting in case of emergencies."

"You're an angel. I'll come in anytime you say, just as soon as I get back. Two weeks from now, whenever."

"I'll get back to you, Opie, okay?"

"Oka-ay. Wholesale, any time you want, Julie. Red's your color, you know. Oops, they're calling me."

"I make it a practice never to use my sources for gain, but thanks anyway. I'll take your advice about red, however. Bye, Opie."

She hung up and then took the receiver in her hand again. When Sara answered, Julie said, "Emergency, emergency, Opie Hart's canceled for tonight. Who've we got for standby that would be incredibly fascinating?"

"You mean in the way of clothes designers? Nobody," Sara said after a long pause. "If you mean fascinating as in Opie, we had him scheduled with one fashion press agent, one fashion writer from *Women's Wear Daily*, and one wealthy woman who wears Opie Harts to the White House. What you'd call an all-around shimmering program."

Julie did not even try to go on the defensive. "The trouble is," she said, "our listeners love that sort of goop. I think they secretly like the glamour stuff far more than listening to life's problems. Don't quote me."

"Especially to Casey Phillips. You sound very calm, Julie. Are you borderline hysteria, ready to scream as soon as you hang up?"

"I wish I had my files sitting here," Julie said. "My mind's a blank. What's a good topic, I mean a really hot one, one that'll hit Casey Phillips right between the eyes?"

"Right between the eyes." Sara was quiet for a moment. Julie heard the baby's laugh in the background. "Ecology?" Sara went on. "How to make a million new jobs out of toxic waste disposal? I was just reading an article...."

"Exciting, Sara, exciting. New, never been tried before. Ecology has grown whiskers, and those whiskers need vacuuming."

"You're borderline hysteria," Sara said calmly. "Want me in earlier? I'll have to get a baby-sitter."

"Nope," said Julie. She nestled the receiver between her shoulder and ear, and stepped out of bed. "I'm a bundle of energy. I'm going to go in now and erase the press agent, erase the fashion reporter, and erase the lady with the White House wardrobe. Then I'm swinging into action."

"Sounds dangerous. I'll come in."

Sara and her writer husband had, enviably, worked out the problems of taking care of their one-year-old and paying their rent on a small uptown apartment. Julie hated having to cut into their routine, but this, she told herself, was war. "How about two o'clock?" she said as a compromise. "I'll pay for the baby-sitter. I hate to do this to you."

"That's radio biz, and I love it. See you at two," Sara said in an ebullient tone.

While dressing for battle—in red—Julie went over her mental list of possible subjects, possible invitees. Important political personages hated being called up at the last minute. They always had full calendars—real or faked. They wanted the exposure but often came prepared with stock arguments, tired ideas and bad tempers.

She would stop in the newsroom first thing before going to her office, to discover any possible news stories that could best be handled by a program like hers.

There were any number of political hacks she could have called, or even behind-the-scenes movers and shakers. But somehow discussions of mugging, graffiti or street people were just more of the same thing. There were no positives on these subjects, only anger and disagreement on how to handle them.

How about art, she thought, or somebody responsible for the buying or selling of it? The head of Lincoln Center, or an opera impresario; a ballerina, or Norman Mailer's editor. Perhaps Norman Mailer himself. No, not Norman Mailer. He was everywhere. She wanted to impress Casey Phillips with her savvy, although for the moment that savvy eluded her.

The one she wanted, she reflected, was E.T.

On the long, pleasant walk downtown from her apartment to the radio station, she found herself still mentally going through her files. She almost missed the fact that the day was warm and sunny with the fresh dew feeling that was a New York specialty on a spring morning. But the honk of a car horn and the whistle of a construction worker drew her up short. Should she be angry or flattered? Flattered, according to Casey Phillips.

There were flowers for sale on the streets, and vegetables lined up on stalls—rich, impressionist still lifes. The women were pretty, the men handsome, and it was great fun to be alive on such a morning and in such a place.

She wanted something earth-shattering on her program, something celebratory of such a day.

It was war, this business with Casey Phillips, but it wasn't world-shaking. It was a minor skirmish with a sexy character she'd made the mistake of going to bed with. Body to body contact with a man whose mouth she had genuinely wanted to kiss perhaps from the moment they met, whose lips she had wanted to cover her body. And it happened. It had been wonderful. It was disaster. She both hated and adored him, had no idea how to handle it intelligently, and was angry about that, too. Perhaps at herself more than him. She continued downtown.

That's what made it all so earth-shattering.

It was eleven o'clock when she stepped out of the express elevator onto the forty-ninth floor of Graff Towers. The receptionist gave her a surprised smile. "Hey, nice to see you, early bird." She nodded in the direction of three people sitting in the corner, talking earnestly together in low voices. "They'd like to see you. I explained you'd be in at four. They're scheduled right now to see Casey Phillips. Can I tell them you're here?"

Julie stared at the trio. Two women, one man, all well groomed and bright-eyed, clearly with some kind of ax to grind. "What are they?"

"L.O.W.," said the receptionist.

Julie stepped closer to the desk. "Yes," she whispered.

The receptionist smiled and handed up a card. "L.O.W. That's their initials. 'Listeners of WRBZ.' They're out for blood."

Julie picked up the card, which was printed in neat letters and bore a brief message. "'Listeners of WRBZ,'" she read. "'Dedicated to keeping good radio on the air.' Lovely, lovely, gorgeous," she said to the receptionist. "I'd love to see them before they meet our station manager," she said, hurrying for the door that led to her office. "Give me a sec or two. I'll buzz you."

On the way she borrowed a chair from the promotion department and hauled it back to her office. That made four, leaving scarcely any room to move around.

She looked quickly through her mail, saw the usual sprinkling of fan letters, the tons of publicity releases, the thank-yous and could-yous she knew the envelopes held, and pushed them all aside. She called the operator for telephone messages and apart from one to call Casey

Phillips the minute she got in, felt all the rest could wait. Casey Phillips could wait, too. She had too much to say to him, and didn't want to say any of it.

She dialed the receptionist. "How long until Mr. Phillips can see the contingent from L.O.W.?"

"Well, so far he's had them sitting out here for a good fifteen minutes. Said he'd get to them soon and to have them wait."

"I hate to see them so uncomfortable out there in that waiting room. Have them come back to my lavish office. And, Amy, possible to scare up some coffee for them? I haven't made any back here yet."

"Possible," said the receptionist. "And if Mr. Phillips wants them while they're in transit?"

"I'll personally escort them to his office."

She hung up and leaned back in her chair, smiling. L.O.W. How clever that name, how artful. Low radio. That should hit Casey Phillips where it hurt. Almost immediately, there was a gentle knock at the door.

She pulled the door open at once, offering a smile that could not conceal her hopefulness, and invited them into her tiny office. War with a vengeance.

There were names to be memorized: Bill MacDonald, Sheila Salisbury, Eleanor Stein. She shook strong hands, noted that each wore a hesitant yet determined smile.

"'Listeners of WRBZ,'" she said, after offering them seats and telling them coffee was on the way. "Sounds terrific." She went behind her desk and sat down, waiting expectantly.

Sheila Salisbury, white-haired with beautiful teeth and startling brown eyes, leaned forward in her chair. "It is terrific, Ms. Garrett."

"Julie. It's the first I've heard of you," Julie said. "Where have you been?"

"Oh, we've been around. It's a long story. We're part of a larger group, 'In Concert.'"

"I've heard of that," Julie stated. "Sort of nationwide watchdog organization that's trying to keep intelligent fare on the radio."

Sheila nodded appreciatively. "The trouble is, we never thought of calling up you people and telling you what a fine job you've done. We just took WRBZ for granted. Now," she added, shrugging, and looking at her companions, "well, let's hope we haven't locked the barn door after the horse has escaped. I'm a lawyer," she went on. "L.O.W. has just been incorporated at my expense. We're temporarily located on Broadway, where I have my offices." She stopped, pulled out a card and handed it across the desk to Julie. "I'm a partner in the law firm of Salisbury, Salisbury and Ebbing."

"And what's the membership of L.O.W.?" Julie asked.

With a smile that took in Julie and her confreres, Sheila said, "'In Concert' has about twenty-five thousand members. L.O.W., well, slightly less than that."

"Twenty," Bill MacDonald put in. "No use hiding the fact."

"Twenty thousand?" Julie asked hopefully.

"Twenty," Eleanor Stein interjected. "But twenty people with clout."

"And the point?" Julie asked, swallowing her disappointment and allowing a warm edge of excitement to begin to come over her anyway. Everything has to begin somewhere.

"The point," Bill MacDonald put in, "is that New York needs WRBZ and we're not about to let it go down the tubes."

"You want to engage in a public relations campaign to gain more members and at the same time to begin proceedings of some kind," Julie said. "Is that it?"

She was rewarded with great smiles of appreciation and Sheila Salisbury raised her hands and applauded Julie. "Precisely. We've come to see Mr. Phillips with a list of demands, but we're so pleased we could talk to you first."

"With twenty listeners you won't have too much clout with Mr. Phillips, or with anyone at Graff Corporation," Julie said.

"Oh, today is fair warning day. We're taking out a full-page ad in the *New York Times* on the weekend." Sheila took a copy of the ad out of her bag and handed it across the desk to Julie, along with several printed sheets.

"A full-page ad in the *Times*!" Julie exclaimed, impressed. "That's pretty expensive."

"We're going to increase our membership. Meanwhile," Sheila said, "the twenty members kicked in the price, along with some moneys from 'In Concert.' A bargain considering we're talking about what we can hear on the airwaves when we want it. We're not at all uncertain about getting it back from our burgeoning membership."

"Pretty sure of yourselves, then," Julie said. She looked at the ad. It was professionally done, which meant one of the twenty was in the advertising business. The headline was bold and was illustrated with an old-fashioned radio set: "The Disappearing Radio Station." The body copy was emphatic, angry, and asked listeners to join L.O.W.

Things were beginning to look better and better. The printed sheets were publicity releases as well as statements of intent. The intent, Julie saw to her delight, was that WRBZ should, must, and would be put back to its original format, if L.O.W. had to go all the way to the FCC in Washington to do it.

Eleanor Stein spoke up. A young, pretty blonde who, Julie thought wryly, would make more points with Casey Phillips than all the ads in the world. "What's happening at WRBZ—ear pollution—could just be against the law. You don't walk in and change a station's character without listener input."

Julie took a deep breath. Her contract with the station called for absolute control over the guests she had. The only restrictions were in the area of libel and poor taste. You can't, she thought, libel a radio station, and as for poor taste, Casey Phillips's program changes qualified for that title better than anything she could think up.

"How would you like to discuss all of this on my program tonight?" she asked.

"Tonight?"

She saw a flush of pleasure creep over their faces, one by one. "Certainly." Her telephone rang. She picked up the receiver and the receptionist cut in at once.

"He's on his way back to pick 'em up. Stormy of eye," she added. Amy was taking literary courses in night school and expected to become a writer of fiction.

"Apologies about the coffee," Julie said, standing up. "Mr. Phillips is coming to collect you personally."

She put down the receiver, feeling an unexpected frisson of fear in the pit of her stomach. She wanted confrontation but on her terms. She heard his footsteps clicking down the corridor and then her door was flung open.

You could have knocked. The words were on the tip of her tongue, but she thought suddenly of the famous French line—*Pas devant les domestiques.* In this case she would have to appear to be absolutely neutral, both to L.O.W. and to the people who paid her salary.

"Here they are," she said gaily. "I stole them from you for just a few minutes." She was stopped by the fierce, frozen look he threw her, and the carefully calm way he came into her small, crowded office.

"Ms. Salisbury, Ms. Stein, Mr. MacDonald," he said at once, ignoring her completely. "Sorry I've kept you waiting. If you'll come back to my office."

Why, he's memorized their names, Julie thought. How very clever of him to impress them. She noted with what could only be the first pangs of jealousy the extra smile he gave Eleanor Stein.

At that moment the office boy came by with the coffee. "Oh," he said, looking in with a sheepish grin. "I was supposed to bring coffee."

"Back in my office," Casey said curtly. He stood at the door. "Ladies, gentleman."

Sheila Salisbury turned to Julie. "Is it true about tonight?" she asked diffidently.

"Very true," Julie said. "I'll expect to see you after your appointment with Mr. Phillips. Oh, incidentally, I was supposed to return your call," she said to Casey.

"So you were."

She received another direct, icy gaze and returned it with a smile that was crushing in its sweetness. It was now war, she reflected, with cold stares at ten paces.

When the door closed and she was faced with her piles of inconsequential mail and telephone messages, Julie felt unexpectedly at loose ends. Somewhere along the line she would have to get some sleep. She sat down and leaned back in her chair, closing her eyes. She thought of brewing some coffee and didn't.

Casey on my mind, she thought, and he wasn't worth the time of day. She wondered, feeling once again the uncalled-for pangs of jealousy, if he would try to make points with Eleanor Stein. Perhaps she was married. People did that sort of thing now and again.

Oh, she thought with a deep sigh, what a fool she had been to have fallen so easily for his tricks. How he must be gloating.

She opened her eyes, picked up the material they had left her and read it through carefully. She had invited the group to appear on her program without any clear idea of their plans. Not exactly the way she usually operated, but in doing battle contingency plans often had to be formulated quickly. She liked what she read. The list of twenty names was impressive: lawyers, writers, artists. They didn't want the format of the station changed and that was enough for Julie.

She reached for her telephone receiver and punched the extension of the station's attorney.

"He's with Mr. Phillips," his secretary informed Julie.

"Have him call me." Well, well, well, she thought. Casey's not taking it lightly if he's asked the station attorney to sit in on the meeting with L.O.W.

Julie knew that she would have to play the devil's advocate that night. She might agree with everything L.O.W. wanted to do, but she had to present their case and WRBZ's case fairly to her audience, and then open up the challenge.

Drew Berkeley. The name surfaced and floated in her mind for a while, a bubble that refused to go away. He was the good-looking gadfly she had dated for a while the previous year. He had wanted to marry her, but Julie had not relished the idea of becoming the third wife of a busy, well-known public relations man who was the image maker for several local and state politicians.

Besides, though she adored him she didn't love him. Once again the visceral feelings aroused in her by Casey Phillips reminded her of what she was waiting for. She wanted both to adore the man she married and love him with a primitive, all-encompassing desire. She wanted to be touched and to have that touch ring through her body, as it had with Casey Phillips. She wanted to be made love to any time of the day or night with an obsessive kind of love that had been missing from her life thus far.

Drew Berkeley, for all his charm and power, had not been that man. Nor was Casey Phillips, dammit.

She picked up her telephone receiver again. She was tired. Being sleepy made her subject to odd speculations and daydreams. Drew Berkeley would be the man to take on the cause of L.O.W., just the man to have on the program along with the three she had engaged. He could always get in a few plugs for his latest product; she would allow him that if he would donate his time to the cause of L.O.W.

The attack on Casey Phillips had begun. Lovely, lovely. What a wonderful day it had turned out, after all.

Julie picked up the telephone receiver once again and punched in Drew Berkeley's number. It was a number she had memorized once and had never tried erasing from her memory.

She and Drew ran into one another on occasion, both at parties and because of her program. He had begun dating almost as soon as their affair had ended, settling at last for beautiful redhead who ran her own interior decorating business. They had married in late winter, Drew even calling Julie beforehand and announcing the fact, as though somehow he must have her approval. She had been relieved, knowing that any regrets she had could now be consigned to history. It would make working with him a lot easier, as well. Now, for instance, when she could use a man of his intelligence and talents.

He was having lunch at his desk, his secretary informed Julie, but put her right through.

"Julie, how's my girl?" Drew said at once in the soft, deep Texas accent that was part of his charm.

"Pretty good. Sorry if I've interrupted lunch."

"The primaries," he said. "That makes it eating-at-my-desk time."

"How's Mrs. Berkeley?"

"Beautiful, happy. She's busy remodeling the apartment, not at all to my taste."

"She *is* an interior decorator," Julie said, and wondered why she felt so smug. She didn't want him to be happy, she supposed, not as happy as he could have been with her. But then, of course, she hadn't wanted him, so it was hardly fair.

"So she is indeed. How are you doing?"

"Splendidly all around, Drew." There was a long pause. They were parrying for no special reason.

"I've wanted to call you," he said.

"I can imagine," she responded gaily. "It's primary time. Time to get your candidates heard if not seen. The truth is, Drew, I could use some angry words and general cussedness."

"Are there problems, then?" he remarked a little hesitantly, "I heard *Night Talk* was being given the old one-two. Pity what they've done to that station. Stop me if I'm wrong, sugar."

Julie took a deep breath. It was just what she wanted to hear, his genuine concern. "I wouldn't go so far as to say *Night Talk* is down the drain, but yes, it's a pity what's happening over here. Drew, would you like to do something about it?"

He laughed, a rich, warm laugh. "Ask me something tough. How much and who do you want to take it up as a political cause?" he asked.

He was grown-up, she thought, not arrogant, not spoiled, not brash, a man who could be reached on tough issues. "You."

He didn't answer at once. She looked up to find Sara there, swooping the unopened envelopes off her desk, and going to work slitting them open.

"Run that by me again," Drew said.

"Drew, it's a long story, but shortened it means I'd like to have you on my show tonight. Don't say no; just listen. There's a group of listeners of WRBZ being formed. You've got to donate your time, *please*..."

"Wait a minute," he said. "Hold on, slow down. I don't know what the hell you're talking about."

"I'm talking about turning the clock back on WRBZ. I want you on the committee of this group of listeners, Drew."

"You're asking me to get on a white horse and I don't even know the critter's name."

"'Listeners of WRBZ,'" Julie said hastily. "L.O.W. for short. It's a real, honest-to-goodness incorporated group of listeners that wants us back the way we wuz."

"My schedule," he began in a lame voice.

"I'm sending everything to you at once," she put in. "Read it over and call me. Could you do that much, please, Drew?"

"I've a three o'clock appointment."

"My program starts at midnight, remember? That's a lifetime away. Drew," she added, "do this for me. I've never asked any favors of you, have I?"

"No," he said thoughtfully, "you haven't."

When she hung up, she looked over at Sara. "You're in early."

"I got my mother to baby-sit. Did you call off the fashion crowd?"

Julie closed her eyes. "No, of course not. I forgot all about them. Could you?"

"Of course I could. What's all this about, anyway? L.O.W. You sound as if you're on to something H-O-T."

"We are. Something stupendous, local radio-speaking, that is. Could you do me a large favor," she added, handing Sara the material L.O.W. had given her. "Read through this first. Then make a couple of copies, and send a set by messenger to Drew Berkeley."

"That's what I'm here for." Sara raised an eyebrow but scuttled out of the office without asking any further questions.

Trying not to bask in what she thought was the correct first step in saving her program, Julie was smiling with triumph when a call came in from the receptionist.

"The contingent from L.O.W. would like to see you."

"Send them back. Are they happy?"

"Look of triumph in their eyes. At least that's what I think it is."

Just as she cradled the receiver, her phone rang again. It was Casey Phillips, his voice cool and without inflection. "I want to see you now." He hung up before she had a chance to answer.

Oh no, she thought, no way. He's trying to cut me off at the pass. No way. She sat at her desk, drumming her fingernails along the top until she heard their footsteps down the corridor. Casey Phillips would have to cool his heels waiting for her.

"Well, you all look quite satisfied," she said, at what she took to be hopeful smiles when they stepped into their office.

"We made our point," MacDonald said.

"He was a little too accommodating," Sheila added. "The station attorney was sitting there the whole time."

"What was the upshot?" Julie asked.

"None at all," Bill put in. "He heard us out, noted that you'd asked us to appear on *Night Talk*, scribbled copious notes—"

"Doodles, if you ask me," Eleanor Stein put in with a smile.

"Well," Julie said, rubbing her hands together in delight, "let's get down to the show. We want to make it a stunner."

"There's just one thing I want to point out," Bill said. "These things don't happen overnight. The FCC moves very slowly and it could take a year or two before a final decision is made. We're planning a fight to the finish."

"Then," Julie said, "let's get moving. I want to be around for the final knockout."

Sara came back in time to listen in on the technical discussion of the program. It was decided that Sheila and Bill would appear on mike to present the case for L.O.W. and that Eleanor Stein would help field extra phone calls if necessary.

Julie then explained about Drew Berkeley, and what they might expect from him.

"Well," she said, walking them out to the elevator, "I think we have a hit on our hands." When the elevator doors closed on them, Julie took herself around to Casey's office. "I'm here," she announced to his secretary, unable to conceal her smile of satisfaction.

"Go right in, but watch out for flying debris." His secretary gave her a broad wink.

Julie didn't stop to consider this last remark, but pushed the door open and marched in, stopping just inside the door. "You wanted to see me?"

"That was ten minutes ago," he told her. "You took your time getting here." He was wearing a denim shirt that deepened the blue of his eyes, adding a tint of violet, eyes that gave no hint at all of what was going on inside him or what had happened between him and Julie. It merely firmed her resolve to keep silent on that subject.

She clenched her hands into tight fists. "You figured it would be nice if I kept the contingent from L.O.W. waiting the way you did. They don't look like people you fool around with, Casey. Get them mad and they'll come in swinging."

"Is that how you read it?" he asked, giving her a patient smile that Julie thought held something lethal in it. It struck her that the space between his desk and the door had widened perceptibly and that she would have to walk a great distance under his angry gaze, just for the sake of dealing with him at close range.

"Simple as ABC," she told him.

"Come in, sit down," he said. "You look as if you're going to cut and run if the going gets tough."

She hesitated for just a moment before coming briskly over to his desk. "*You* wanted to see *me*," she reminded him.

"So I did. Incidentally, red's your color." Then, before she had a chance to react, he gave her a good-natured smile and waved her to a chair. "That's MacDonald, Salisbury and Stein for tonight. And baby makes four. I'm Baby."

The news staggered her, but she kept her eyes unwaveringly on his. She had no doubt at all that he had a couple of aces up his sleeve. "I'll stand, thank you," she said with exaggerated politeness. "And that's terrific news. I'd love to have you on tonight. It's what I've wanted for a long time."

"Have you now?"

"If you don't remember, then your memory is distressingly short."

"Oh, I remember the things that are important to me," he told her. "All else is dross."

"Of course, Ms. Stein won't be on the program," she told him.

"Pity," he said.

"Instead we're going to have Drew Berkeley."

He drew his brows together and then at last said, "I'm new to this part of the country. You'll have to refresh my memory. Drew Berkeley. Is he someone I'm supposed to be afraid of?"

"Drew Berkeley of the Texas Berkeleys," she said sweetly. "Oil, I think. He runs a public relations firm that handles politicians and people of that ilk. Takes up causes, too."

"I see. This is one cause that his clients will leech onto."

"I believe the word, Casey, is latch."

"On the contrary, Julie, I meant what I said. Leech."

"It sounds as if the battle is heating up," she remarked. "Wonderful. Think of all the publicity it's going to generate."

"I can see the editorials in the *Times* and *Daily News*. Quote, 'Twenty Listeners Girding for Radio Battle of a Lifetime,' end quote." Casey snorted derisively.

Julie smiled. His sarcasm required no response. She had the odd feeling that the whole business was making him uneasy. What she wanted to do was make him a lot more so. To do that she had to refrain from taking him on in an essentially empty battle of wits.

She turned and went rapidly over to the door. "Show time is midnight, Casey. We like our guests to be there well ahead of time—you know, in case of any last-minute glitches, things like that."

"Oh, I'll be there," he said. "Wild horses couldn't keep me away."

You know the thrill of escaping to a world of PASSION...SENSUALITY ...DESIRE...SEDUCTION... and LOVE FULFILLED...

Escape again...with 4 FREE novels and

**get more great Silhouette Desire® novels
—for a 15-day FREE examination—
delivered to your door every month!**

Silhouette Desire offers you real-life drama and romance of successful women in charge of their lives and their careers, women who face the challenges of today's world to make their dreams come true. They are not for everyone; they're for women who want a sensual, provocative reading experience.

These are modern love stories that begin where other romances leave off. They take you *beyond* the others and into a world of love fulfilled and passions realized. You'll share precious, private moments and secret dreams...experience every whispered word of love, every ardent touch, every passionate heartbeat. And now you can enter the unforgettable world of Silhouette Desire each and every month.

FREE BOOKS

You can start today by taking advantage of this special offer— 4 new Silhouette Desire romances (a $9.00 Value) *absolutely FREE,* along with a FREE Folding Umbrella and Mystery Gift. Just fill out and mail the attached order card.

AT-HOME PREVIEWS, FREE DELIVERY

After you receive your 4 free books and free gifts, every month you'll have the chance to preview 6 more Silhouette Desire novels *—as soon as they are published!* When you decide to keep them, you'll pay just $11.70 (a $13.50 Value), *with no additional charges of any kind and at no risk!* You can cancel your subscription at any time just by dropping us a note. In any case, the first 4 books and both FREE gifts are yours to keep.

EXTRA BONUS

When you take advantage of this offer, we'll also send you the Silhouette Books Newsletter FREE with each book shipment. Every informative issue features news on upcoming titles, interviews with your favorite authors, and even their favorite recipes.

Get a Folding Umbrella & Mystery Gift Free!

EVERY BOOK YOU RECEIVE WILL BE A BRAND-NEW FULL-LENGTH NOVEL!

Escape with 4 Silhouette Desire novels (a $9.00 Value) and get a Folding Umbrella & Mystery Gift Free!

Silhouette Desire®

Silhouette Books, 120 Brighton Rd., P.O. Box 5084, Clifton, NJ 07015-9956

☐ YES! Please send me my four SILHOUETTE DESIRE novels FREE, along with my FREE Folding Umbrella and Mystery Gift, as explained in this insert. I understand that I am under no obligation to purchase any books.

NAME _____
(please print)

ADDRESS _____

CITY _____ STATE _____ ZIP _____

Terms and prices subject to change.
Your enrollment is subject to acceptance by Silhouette Books.

SILHOUETTE DESIRE is a registered trademark.

CED066

Why, she wondered, after throwing him another smile and stepping out of his office, did she feel that although they were twenty-five or thirty feet apart, he had whispered the words softly, seductively in her ear?

Six

Drew Berkeley called back almost immediately after receiving and reviewing the packet of notes on L.O.W. that Julie had sent him. "You certainly ask a lot of a man," he said in a friendly, joking tone.

"What do you think of the group?" she asked at once.

"I've heard of 'In Concert,'" he told her. "Friend of mine handles their promotion without a fee. They began some years back in Washington, D.C., of all places, when the one and only classical music station was about to be sold down the Potomac. They saved the station and a loosely built national watchdog group resulted, but I guess you know all that. If L.O.W. is an offshoot, then they have some heavy interest backing them. And cases like WRBZ have gone before the FCC and won."

"Drew, I've only one question. Can I count on you tonight to back up my panel?"

"I like your funky little station, Julie; you know that."

"Just what I wanted to hear, Drew. Question repeated. Can I count on you tonight?"

"I'm no expert on either the FCC or on besieged radio stations."

"You're a listener and you're articulate. That's all you have to be." And a first-class debater, she thought. He'd step all over Casey.

He was quiet for a moment and then said, "I'll do what I can, but I can't get there before eleven-thirty."

"I'm grateful for whatever time you can give us, Drew." She was actually pleased that he would be late. Somehow she didn't want him sitting around with Casey Phillips, and she couldn't have said why.

But at eleven o'clock, just when she expected the panel from L.O.W. to arrive, her intercom buzzed.

"Drew Berkeley to see you," Sara told her.

"Oh damn, he's early."

Sara gathered up her papers and went to the door. "I'll bring him back and then I'll be in the studio."

Julie nodded absentmindedly. She should have remembered that about Drew. He liked doing the unexpected. It threw people off balance. She remembered how she had almost confused his remarkable ability to persuade with a real belief in what he was selling. But then again he was doing her a favor, and she needed all the help she could get to ward off Casey Phillips tonight. It might, she thought, a smile hovering on her lips, even be fun to watch those two square off against each other.

She was on her feet when he appeared at her doorway, her hand outstretched to avoid the hug and kiss she knew he expected.

"Julie," he said, drawing out her name. He ignored her hand and grabbed her, pulling her close. His lips were cool against her cheek as she turned her face away.

"Same old Julie," he whispered. "Never could get you to hold still for the count."

"Hey, you're a married man," she said, moving adroitly away from him.

"That never stopped me before."

He had put on a little weight, but it only added a bit more force to an already imposing frame. He was a big man and he used his body in the confident way of men who spend their lives gazing over the heads of other people.

"You're looking good, Drew," she said, drawing up a chair for him. She retreated quickly behind her desk while he sat down. "I'm glad to see you, really. The last time was..."

"Exactly one year ago tomorrow," he said. "Aside from those brief encounters at parties where I never got a chance to talk to you."

"The panel should be here any minute," she said hastily, not wanting the conversation to continue on a personal level.

"You've been avoiding me, haven't you?" he remarked, reaching into his jacket pocket for a cigarette.

"You're sitting in my office. Here I am." She forced herself to sound bright. She hadn't really given him much thought once they had broken up. "As a matter of fact, I've wanted to call you and Toni, have you over for drinks...."

"We had a good thing going," he said, interrupting her once again. "You just got stubborn." He slowly stood up and came around to her desk, perching on the edge so that his large frame seemed to box her in. He reached out and put his hand under her chin, lifting it up. "Your call today was just what I was waiting for."

She inhaled deeply, wishing fervently that her phone would ring or that Sara would come dashing in. "Drew, I hope you're not going to be sentimental," she said. She put her hand up to brush his arm away.

"My wife's a great gal," he said, "don't get me wrong." He bent forward and she knew that if she didn't act at once, his mouth would descend on hers.

"The door," she said in sheer desperation.

"Damn, it's always the door." He turned and Julie drew in her breath sharply. Casey had come in, and was standing in the doorway, his face dark and expressionless. His eyes moved over them both in a slow arc.

Julie got quickly to her feet, pushing her chair back, hearing it roll along the linoleum-covered floor to bang against the cabinet behind her.

"Oh, Casey, glad you're here," she said, swallowing her embarrassment and smiling. "This is Drew Berkeley. Drew, Casey Phillips, our station manager. You're going to be pitted against one another tonight."

Drew came out from behind her desk, wearing a broad, charming smile, his hand outstretched. "Glad to meet you, Casey."

Drew was going to play all sides until the program began, she thought, watching them shake hands, feeling the heaviness of the air between them as they sized one another up. Casey might win or lose the debate but, as station manager, he was a comer. Drew was already figuring out how to use him.

She wondered for a terrible moment whether she had done the right thing in calling Drew.

When the intercom buzzed it was the guard at the reception desk announcing her other guests. Well, it was too late now. She had started it, and it was up to her to carry it through.

They sat around the large, square studio table with Sara directing from the control booth, and Eleanor Stein there to help field the call-ins.

Julie opened her mike and spoke to Sara. "About the call-ins. Try to get our listeners' ages, their incomes, and what they do for a living."

"You're leading with your left," Casey said to her.

"Am I? I think I know what I'm doing."

He eased himself into the chair opposite her, forcing Julie to look at him every time she raised her eyes. It was a disconcerting and deliberate move on his part; his amused, mocking expression dared her to make a fool of him.

The talk heated up from the moment Julie introduced her guests over the air. She had brought together four articulate people who were experienced enough not to trip over anyone else's words, or to force some kind of foolish confrontation.

It was Sheila Salisbury who led off with a simple, declarative sentence, summing up L.O.W.'s aims. "Leave well enough alone, is all 'Listeners of WRBZ' are asking. *Leave well enough alone.* It took this station fifteen years to achieve clever, offbeat programming that attracts a wide, varied audience and three months for its new owners almost to wipe it out. Thanks to such manipulation, a segment of this city's population is without a listening home, so to speak. 'Listeners of WRBZ,' called L.O.W. for short, believes it has a case for this disenfranchised audience. It's a case we'll take before the FCC in the very near future. Meanwhile," she added, her eyes raised in a question to Julie, "can I give the address of L.O.W., in case your listeners want to write us and join?"

"Of course, go right ahead, Sheila."

Casey reached out, fingered the mike as though he were going to say something, and then sat back.

In an effort to appear neutral, Julie, in addressing a question to Bill MacDonald, knew she was opening the floor for a free-for-all. "Mr. MacDonald, we know it should be fair radio, we know it should be free radio for its listeners, but we also know that someone has to pay the bills. My salary, for instance. Isn't it the first duty of management to seek out the largest possible audience? After all, advertisers look at demographics and numbers before they'll buy time."

She looked up. Casey bent his head in acknowledgment.

MacDonald cleared his throat and then leaned slightly forward. "There are thousands of listeners being shunted aside because we don't seem to fall into the correct demographic patterns. We're too old, or we don't make enough money or live in the right places. About the only thing going for us, apparently, is that we have ears."

Casey signaled Julie with a nod and Julie introduced him to her audience, knowing that his attractive, resonant voice would intrigue and mellow them.

"I'd say you had a point, Bill," he began, "if our station were the only place in town for the kind of listening you like. But there are other stations covering the odd-man-out audience in the city. Public radio, for one. In fact, there are two in this area, as well as several college stations. Plus all the classical music you can eat on two stations."

Drew Berkeley shook his head. "Casey, that's a little like saying one Broadway show should suffice for all the theatergoing audience, or one opera house, or one book for the general population. WRBZ found its audience, satisfied its audience, and should be satisfying it until the next century. By your own count, one more rock station in a city where most of the stations cater to rock listeners is just another attempt to ruin the eardrums of the young." The sarcasm in his tone was heavy and Julie threw him a grateful smile.

Sheila Salisbury joined in. "Are you playing music you really like, Casey?" she asked in a very sweet voice.

Casey cast a murderous glance at Julie, but Julie only shrugged and smiled. It was an innocent question, and one Julie had not put her up to.

"I think you've a very odd notion of who the listener to contemporary popular music is, Ms. Salisbury," Casey said, adroitly avoiding her question. "We have a whole group out there who arrived on the scene in the sixties and seventies. They're adults, yuppies, no longer puppies."

"Yuppies or puppies is beside the point, isn't it," Drew said. "They're the ones with the money—am I right, Casey?"

"They're our target audience, Drew," Casey said. "We have to move with the times, as you well know. WRBZ has flooded the airwaves with question and answer programs, advice to the lovelorn, husband and wife teams arguing at breakfast, and," he added with a nod at Julie, "present company excepted, talk shows that keep recirculating the same people and the same ideas from radio to television and back again. It's old hat and nobody wants it."

Sheila said, her voice full of good humor, "Mr. Phillips, I suspect you never even listen to WRBZ," she said.

Bill MacDonald added, "Your description of the station's programming doesn't quite fit what we know of it."

Casey laughed. "I ought to know about it, considering how much of it I had to bring up-to-date."

The air was electric, so much so that Julie did not want to recognize Sara's frantic signal to read the commercial.

But commercials, she thought wryly, were what it was all about. She picked up the copy and read it through carefully, emphasizing each word and even repeating the product name more times than she needed to.

When she was through, Casey spoke up, and the humor in his voice was obvious. "Fine product, that."

"I don't believe we should turn our backs on advertisers," Julie said. "I think I made myself clear on that point."

"Graff Corporation," Casey said, exasperated now, "never received a mandate to lose money."

"Mr. Berkeley," Julie said, as Drew opened his mouth to speak. The program was getting out of hand and she wondered if the audience could recognize each voice without her identifying it.

"You're reaching for the lowest common denominator, Casey. There are people who want programs that offer insight on the news, financial reporting that's more than just surface announcements, and yes, talk shows that aren't Hollywood gossip. We've heard the mayor say things on *Night Talk* that he would never say on television."

"Right," Casey said. "At two o'clock in the morning it's safe to say anything with a listening audience of nursing mothers up for the two o'clock feeding, and half a dozen night watchmen all over town." He sat bolt upright and examined each member of the panel in turn. "I have a mandate not only to upgrade the programs on this station, but to save money and to bring in more advertising revenue. I can't do that by keeping the same old routine."

"Speaking of money," Drew said, throwing a wide smile at Julie, "I hear you're getting a pretty hefty salary, plus a percentage of the advertising profits."

For a moment there was a heavy silence and as Julie moved to give another commercial, Casey spoke up in a

quiet, clear voice. "My tail is on the line as much as anyone's. If I don't produce good, exciting radio, I'm out.
And that's the way it should be."

Julie reached out and touched Sheila's arm. There was
something personal going on between the two men and she
wanted Sheila to jump in, but the other woman merely
shook her head. Drew had apparently taken time out of his
busy day to research Casey Phillips. *That* was the miracle,
but then Julie knew it was why she had instinctively called
him.

Drew was talking in his calm, authoritative way. "Apart
from the expensive renovation of the studios," he went on,
"the station advertising department has a huge, shall we
say, entertainment budget. Enough, from what I gather, to
sink the national debt. Oh, and I mustn't forget to in-
clude trips abroad to learn what our friends in Europe are
doing radio-wise, for the head of the station, Norbert
Graff."

"Your information is all wrong, friend," Casey said. "I
can't imagine where you got it."

"From an impeccable source."

Casey caught Julie with a look of pure fury. She thought
with a sickening sensation that he believed she had told
Drew about his salary. She didn't know the first thing
about it. For a moment she had a feeling that Casey and
Drew were fighting over her, then the feeling was gone.
Stupid thought, one that would only come in the heat of
the moment. "Suppose we take our first phone call," she
interposed quickly.

She looked into the control booth at Sara, hoping that
she and Eleanor Stein had kept an accurate head count of
who was for a station change, and who against.

"Hello," she said, switching to the first call. "You're on
the air."

"Hello, Julie?" The voice wavered for a moment and then went on. "I'm Simon from Westchester."

"Hello, Simon. Go ahead."

"I just want to say I think you're great, and if they let you go, I'm going to come down and picket the place myself."

"Well, thank you, Simon." She cast a quick glance at Casey but he merely gave her a smile of supreme confidence. "Tell me, Simon," she went on, "what do you think of the new WRBZ?"

"I think it stinks. I'm a truck dispatcher and I sit in one of those little boothlike offices all night, you know?"

"Ah-hah. Go on."

"Well, listen, I like rock music, don't get me wrong. I got dozens of stations to tune in if I want that. But WRBZ...you want to hear voices in the middle of the night, saying something, you know?"

"I know, Simon. Appreciate your call."

She disconnected and had to force herself not to throw a smug look in Casey's direction. Instead she satisfied herself with a smile at Drew Berkeley, who winked back at her.

"If I might say a word to your listeners, Julie," Drew began.

"Drew Berkeley," she said, automatically informing her listeners who the speaker was.

"Our friend Simon from Westchester makes two points in favor of smart radio. One, if he wants rock, he has access to it. Two, WRBZ is his choice when he wants to use his gray matter."

"As I've said before," Casey put in, "there are other stations for the relatively few Simons in New York who want call-in programs."

"Thank you, Mr. Phillips," Julie said. "We'll take another call now."

She closed her eyes briefly and wished she had never become involved. It was going to be a long, long two hours.

Later, at the one o'clock newsbreak, Julie was beginning to wonder whether the headache she felt coming on would explode soon. There would be a five-minute newsbreak and another five minutes for commercials. "Shall we all get up for a seventh-inning stretch?" she asked the panel.

Sheila stretched happily. "Wonderful."

"You can go outside into the corridor if you want to stretch your legs," she suggested.

She waited while Drew, with an arm on both MacDonald's and Salisbury's shoulders, directed them firmly outside. A powwow, Julie thought; not a bad idea. She turned her back on Casey, who was getting slowly to his feet, and headed for the control booth.

"How's it going?" she asked Sara, who silently handed her a yellow memo pad.

"Read it and weep," Sara said. "The calls for and against," she said. "We've been clobbered."

"What are you talking about?" Julie asked, hearing the alarm in her own voice. "The callers so far have been evenly divided."

"The ones that went on the air," Sara said. "It just worked out that way, Julie. We've kept an accurate count, unfortunately. But they're coming in two-to-one for good old rock. Everyone who called said they were fans of yours, but that they felt the general programming was headed in the right direction."

"I don't believe it," Julie said, checking the list, but the numbers were there. The age range of most callers was from youth to middle age, and their incomes were right there for Casey's plucking. She felt no satisfaction that her fans were loyal. Even if it were possible, she didn't want to be the only voice left on WRBZ.

"Oh, damn," she said.

Sara gave her a warning shake of her head. Julie didn't even have to turn to know that Casey had come into the control booth.

"What have we here?" he said, reaching for the memo pad.

"I haven't finished studying it yet," she said tightly.

"Go ahead, by all means." He took a step back and gazed at her with an amused smile.

"It doesn't give us much information," she said, slipping the pad under her arm. "There were about fifty calls."

"That's thirty more listeners than I thought you had. Congratulations."

Sara coughed and turned to Eleanor Stein, who was still on the telephone fielding calls. "We've got six minutes before we're back on the air. Maybe I'd better hustle up some coffee."

"Great idea," Casey said. "And while you're at it, an aspirin or two. I think your boss is going to need it."

"You didn't seem so sure of yourself when you were arguing with Drew Berkeley," Julie said.

She turned around and stopped Sara as she was going out of the control booth. "How's it going?" she asked in a low voice. "Generally, I mean."

"Fantastic. It's a prizefight, all right. Drew Berkeley against Casey Phillips. I've got the coffee machine going in the newsroom. Be back in a second."

Julie turned to find that Casey had picked up the earphones and was listening to one of the calls. When he put them down, the cold glint in his eye was unnerving. "Let's see the numbers, Julie. You can't hide them forever."

"They don't prove anything, yet," she said. "When we get the message out, you'll hear from our supporters."

"That bad, eh?" He took the pad away from her, then deliberately did not look at it, handing it silently back to Eleanor Stein. "I won't bother looking it over. The expression on your face tells everything."

"What did you do," she asked hotly, aware that both Eleanor and the engineer were listening, "get everyone including your mother to call tonight?"

"Oh, Julie," he said, shaking his head and pretending to be hurt, "you fight hard and mean when your back is against the wall. You have to learn to give in with a certain amount of grace."

She turned and opened the door to the studio. "What are you talking about?" she threw back at him. "I didn't start this particular ball rolling. Although I would have, if I'd thought about it. This afternoon I didn't know L.O.W. from a hole in the wall. They formed of their own volition; they came to see you without any advice from me."

"Funny," he said, "this business with Drew Berkeley. He didn't know our friends Salisbury and MacDonald when he showed up here tonight. Interesting. Drew Berkeley of the Texas Berkeleys, head of his own public relations firm, an old buddy of yours I haven't any doubt, especially after that little scene in your office."

"And if you'd announce yourself instead of sneaking up on people, maybe you wouldn't misconstrue what you think you see."

"You're right. I should have let that kiss deepen."

"He didn't—" she began, feeling her face grow hot. No, she thought, he wasn't going to make her lose her temper.

"He's an old friend," Julie said in a slow, calm voice. "And he has an interest in what happens to this station."

"Friend?" Casey moved closer. "I'd say his only interest in WRBZ is you."

She moved away quickly and snapped, "I don't want to discuss this any longer, Casey. You've no right to get so personal."

"Haven't I?"

She took in a deep, impatient sigh, wondering whether the sound was on in the control booth. It was all getting out of hand and she looked up gratefully when Sara came in bearing a tray of coffee, Julie's guests trooping in after her.

"Three minutes," Sara said.

Julie stepped out into the empty corridor, wanting to leave it all behind her for a few moments. She stood leaning back against the cool wall, her eyes closed.

Then she was aware of Casey, his hand above her against the wall, closing her in. "There's one thing more," he said in a low voice. "I want you to tell your gang of malcontents that I don't bow to the pressure of a couple of late-night sleepless freaks. They'd be better advised to turn their attention to something they can really affect, like shelters for retired horses, or whether the glue on the back of stamps is harmful to your health."

"It's your contempt that's going to do you in," Julie said, moving out from under his arm.

He grabbed her shoulders and held her back. "It's not contempt, Julie. It's hard-gained knowledge of what works and what doesn't work anymore." His voice suddenly softened. "You're taking the whole thing personally. I want to try and pound some sense into you."

"Pound is the operative word." She turned. The On the Air sign over the door blinked. "We're on the air in a minute."

"Dammit, listen to me." His fingers bit roughly into her flesh. "We're two professionals. You should be able to separate your work from your private life."

What were they arguing about? she wondered. Something else. The night in Connecticut, they way they had made love, and the way she had run away. "Maybe you can do that, but I can't," she said. "You have some strange notion that you can sandbag me here at the station. Once outside in the fresh air, all you have to do is put the make on me and we can rush off somewhere to bill and coo."

He seemed startled by her words and she flushed. Perhaps she had gone too far.

"I'm not going to let this happen, Julie," he said slowly. "Somehow I'm going to prove that you're wrong about me."

"Your powers of persuasion are probably second to none," she said, pulling away from him, "but save your energy for the fight ahead. You'll need it." She turned and walked quickly back into the studio, aware of the tension she brought with her.

Seven

Afternoon, Sara." Julie threw her bag down on her desk, and went right for the coffee machine. "Lovely day, isn't it? I think."

"Afternoon, Julie. Catch up on your sleep?"

"Fifteen minutes here and there through the long, agonizing night. You?"

"Good enough, considering there's a baby around the house. Why fifteen minutes here and there, though? I don't get it. The program was a success; it was lively and interesting. Your guests were cleveer, and L.O.W. made its radio debut. Quote, you heard it here first, folks, on Julie Garrett's *Night Talk*, end quote. You should have been thrilled."

"Yup. The kind of thrill that kept me awake for hours, going over every inch of it." Julie sank down in her chair and gulped her coffee. "Ah, medicine," she said.

It was four o'clock, fourteen hours after the program on which Casey Phillips had made his clever mark—and it still rankled. She had not stayed after the program to congratulate him for winning the call-in war, but had hurried from the studio with her other guests, grabbing a cab with Sara immediately afterward, and thereby avoiding Drew's offer to see her home. She had pleaded exhaustion, but the unnatural high she was on had kept her mind churning through the long night.

Sara turned to her and with a serious look in her eyes said, "I know what's got your back up, Julie. Casey Phillips won that little skirmish, didn't he?"

Julie took a few seconds before answering, somehow anxious to seem sane and rational when what she really wanted to do was to pick up the paperweight and throw it at the door merely to hear the sound of crashing glass.

"Sara," she said at last, "he talked faster, brasher, and maybe smoother than anyone else. Dulcet tones, that's all. If you ask me, I'd say he loaded the call-ins with friends," she added after a moment. "I wish I'd thought of that."

"No, you don't." Sara turned back to her typewriter and began pounding on it. "I believe he meant what he said and obviously your listeners did, too."

Julie glanced thoughtfully at her. Casey Phillips was leaving his mark everywhere, even in her tiny office, setting off a quiet quarrel between assistant and boss. They were too civilized, Sara and she, to let it escalate, but it left a bad feeling in the air.

Still, she found she couldn't let Sara's remark go unanswered, not when it came to Casey Phillips. "All he'd need would be one friend with a portfolio of funny voices and a bunch of quarters. Casey would do that sort of thing, even for a lark."

"Ah, you know him that well?" asked Sara, giving her a discerning look.

Julie flushed. "Anyway, it's not a popularity contest, who gets the most calls."

"Really? I thought that's just what it was. Listener input, etcetera, etcetera. Demographics, etcetera and so on. This many callers representing that many listeners. Come on, Julie," Sara added, "Casey asking his friends to call in and support him? That's a big assumption and it's not fair. He was very convincing in his arguments. The station programming is a funky little house party and Graff wants it to become a moneymaking operation. This is America and hooray for the profit motive. Casey doesn't need to call up a dozen friends to make his point for him, or one person in a monkey suit."

"You're stuck on Casey Phillips, too, I suppose," Julie remarked almost savagely. She began sifting, without much interest, through her mail. "Where are the ratings sheets? Shouldn't they be in today?" Without waiting for an answer, she went on about Casey. "I don't mean love-struck, either. That wide, blue-eyed look he gives has enough wattage to light up downtown New York." She was tired, angry, and beginning to wonder whether it was all worth it. "Sara, it's the meat on your table we're talking about," she said.

"I'm a vegetarian."

"Then it's the cauliflower on your table I'm talking about, Sara."

Sara laughed, but Julie understood quite well what the laugh meant. "I'm tired," she sighed by way of apology.

"Of the program, Julie?"

"Maybe."

"I'm betting your contract will be renewed. I'm betting that L.O.W. will win a stay of execution and the funky little station will stay on the air for good and all. How's that for prognostication?''

Julie relaxed and threw her a grateful smile. "Very enlightening. Let's not talk about Casey Phillips for the next six months, shall we?"

"Well, we won't have to for the next couple of weeks, anyway. He left for Minneapolis this morning."

Keep talking was Julie's first shocked reaction. "Well, we can thank heaven for little things," she said, aware of the unnaturally harsh tone of her voice. "How come you know all these things?"

"I met his secretary in the ladies' room."

"Ah, of course, the grapevine." She smiled across at Sara. He had left without a word. Two weeks. She should have been happy about it, but she wasn't. The heel, she thought. He should have sent a message somehow, and not through his secretary in the ladies' room.

"Now, about tonight's program," she said busily to Sara to hide her confusion. "How does it line up?"

"Straight as an arrow. Everybody's on."

The sudden jangling of the telephone seemed like an imposition on the quiet air. For a moment they both sat and looked at one another, as though they were in a haunted house and had just been visited by a ghostly screech.

Julie laughed in relief. Anything was better than thinking about Casey. "I'll get it," she said hurriedly, reaching for the phone. She immediately recognized the voice at the other end as that of the secretary to Norbert Graff, who was chief executive of operations for the Graff Corporation. In her pleasant, yet vaguely imperative tone, she said, "Mr. Graff would like to see you in five minutes' time, if that's convenient."

Julie looked across at Sara with a worried frown. "Yes, yes, of course, I'll be right there."

She hung up and said to Sara, "I'm due on the fifty-second floor. Norbert Graff, the big cheese, wants to see me. What do you think that means?"

Sara smiled brightly. "He wants to renew your contract, honey. That's all."

"My, we're full of good words today."

"Think positive, Julie. It's the only way to get through this life."

Graff's office was huge, yet homey; an English baronet's dark study complete with working fireplace and miles of untouched books on mahogany shelves. There was a pleasant scent of cigar smoke and cedar in the cool air that greeted her. Outside was a terrace, and beyond that a direct view of the Empire State Building, monolithic and serene against the clear downtown skyline.

Graff was a small man, dominated by his desk and all the valuable accoutrements of success; paintings, sculpture, furniture, none of which seemed to fit him very well. Still, he was the director of operations of the company that had been started by his grandfather, with billions of dollars in assets. Being in his presence made Julie very nervous.

He came around his desk to greet her, a huge cigar in his hand, and Julie realized that she had never seen him without one. He was rotund, dressed in an elegant suit of British cut. Rimless aviator glasses gave his round, baby face an unexpectedly rakish look. "Coffee?" he said at once. His voice was a rough growl, as though he had grown up on the docks. He nodded at his secretary, who withdrew, Julie imagined, to bring the coffee, although she hadn't said she wanted any.

"You wanted to see me," she stated, and then was sorry at once for the obviousness of her remark.

"Sit down, sit down," he said expansively, pushing a chair around for her. "Here, where you get a good view. Everybody loves that view."

Julie dutifully took a seat in an upholstered Queen Anne chair, sitting at the edge, noting her own tenseness. Graff went back behind his desk and sat down in a huge, suede-covered chair, wearing a smile that could not quite conceal a certain tough determination.

"What's this about L.O.W.?" he asked without ceremony. "That's not something you've cooked up personally, is it?"

The remark, though unexpected, didn't offend Julie. With a little imagination, that's just what it would seem. "Oh, Mr. Graff," she said, offering him a hurt smile, "you don't really believe that, do you?"

"I can't say what I believe," he said, pausing to light his cigar. "Here this organization comes out of the blue, threatening to take us to the FCC and you put them on your program without so much as a by-your-leave."

"Casey Phillips was on the program as well," she pointed out. "The station attorney was present at the initial meeting that Mr. Phillips had with them. L.O.W. is a fait accompli and it's no use pretending they don't exist."

"Twenty listeners!"

"Part of a nationwide group that considers itself a watchdog of the airwaves."

"'In Concert,'" he said disdainfully.

"And a full-page ad in next Sunday's *Times*."

"They're wasting their time and money."

"Well," Julie said, "we'll know sooner or later."

"Tell me," Graff said, leaning across his desk and waving the cigar in the air, "what do you think is going to happen to your program?"

The question took her aback. Even Casey had been less than straightforward when it came to what the company's plans for *Night Talk* were.

"I think my program pays for itself. It has a list of steady advertisers that show no signs of deserting me. I'd like to think *Night Talk* will mark its quarter-century history with WRBZ, Mr. Graff."

"Well," he said, leaning back in his chair and squinting up at the blue smoke that trailed from his cigar, "I like unvarnished optimism. Radio," he went on in a portentous tone, "is a wonderful invention. The only thing not invented was how to put it over the airwaves without paying for the privilege. Announcers, engineers, gophers. They all like to be paid at week's end."

"Goodwill is also money," Julie said a little feebly.

"Is it now?" He gazed at her long and seriously, the light that reflected off his glasses giving him a surprised look.

"Public service," she added.

"We're not in the public service business," he remarked in an unexpectedly sour tone.

The door opened and a steward came in bearing cups of fragrant coffee. Julie dutifully waited while it was served, reflecting on the rewards of power.

When he was gone, Graff picked up his cup and sipped quietly for a moment. Then he said, "Media is where it's at, right now, profitably speaking, and WRBZ must go aggressively after its share of the metropolitan listening audience. Now, we haven't come on the way some corporations do; we haven't stopped intellectual broadcasting one day and blasted the air with all rock the next. We've been easing our way into our new audience's life, and giving the old plenty of time to shop around for other stations that will suit their taste. And there *are* others; we both know that. But we're planning a big advertising campaign for six months from now. We didn't figure on 'Listeners of WRBZ,' and we're going to take them on strong."

"Excuse me," Julie said, "but I would like to point out that even if the FCC hears the arguments in the next month or so, a final decision may not be reached for over a year."

Graff took a pull at his cigar, which he then examined for ash. "We're quite familiar with the ways and byways of the FCC. Meanwhile, that ragged little group that calls itself L.O.W. doesn't need us to give it any more publicity, Julie, and I'd take it kindly if you kept them off the air."

He smiled at her, a smile that seemed to underline his embarrassment at having to lay down the law. Oh, he's in charge all right, Julie thought. The soft hand with the strength of a hidden threat behind it. No wonder he hired Casey Phillips. They were as alike as two bugs in a rug.

"My contract gives me the right to take on whom I please," she began.

"So far we haven't gone over your contract with a fine-tooth comb."

"My lawyer has, Mr. Graff."

He referred to a file folder that was sitting on his desk. "Let's see, the contract has a way to go before it's up," he said.

"Yes."

His smile was beamed at her once again. "Well, we really don't want to bore our listeners with too much of a good thing, do we?"

Julie put her coffee cup down on the little table beside her chair. "Mr. Graff," she said, standing up and returning his smile with a small one of her own, "I never like to bore my listeners. I think last night's program was the highlight of the season. The battle lines were drawn, our listeners are taking sides, and we know from the way the board lit up that we have a pretty good following." Casey must have read the figures to him she told herself, but she decided to tough it out and act as if L.O.W. had won the opening round. "However, I don't believe in gilding the lily, Mr. Graff. I might never have L.O.W. on my program again—not because I'd be afraid to, but because the issue is out in the open where it should be. My listeners want variety, and that's just what I give them." She stopped, aware of the lecturing tone in her voice and the fact that her knees were unaccountably shaking.

He stood up quickly and came around his desk. "Well then," he said in a good-humored tone, "the months ahead should be fascinating ones." He took her elbow and steered her toward the door. "I find conversations like this very enlightening."

"Any time you want to discuss possible subjects for my program, I'd be glad to hear them." They shook hands warmly, but it was only when she was back in her office that Julie allowed herself to think of what he had said. The months ahead should be fascinating ones. Months. Not years. There was no doubt about it. When her contract was up, they intended to write finis under *Night Talk*.

It was close to six-thirty when Julie turned to Sara and said, "I'm skipping out for an hour or two. What are you planning on doing for dinner?" She had promised to stop at Sheila Salisbury's office to go over the results of the program, and she realized that she was only too glad to get away from her small, stifling office for a while.

Sara looked as if she wanted to ask a question, but then changed her mind. "I could dash off home and have dinner with Mike, see Sandy, and then get back here by seven-thirty, eight.''

"Fine all around," Julie said. She stood up, came out from behind her desk and stretched. They had put in two good hours of work, answering mail and handling telephone calls. They had begun to compile a list of questions to ask that night's guests and would finish well before the first one showed up. She went over to the mirror that stood on the file cabinet and ran a comb through her hair. She wore a wide-sleeved beige linen dress that still looked fresh and crisp on her slender figure. She freshened her lipstick, grabbed her bag and went quickly out the door.

It was eight o'clock when Julie arrived back at the studio. She and Sheila had gone out for a bite to eat after their meeting and when Julie got off at the forty-ninth floor of Graff Towers, she was well satisfied with the interest that the program on L.O.W. had generated. Drew Berkeley had definitely agreed to come on board and he and Sheila had already begun mapping out publicity strategy.

"Hey, where've you been?" the receptionist asked when she saw Julie.

"How come you're working late?" Julie asked.

"I agreed to take the five to ten shift. I need the extra money if I'm ever going to finish school."

"Welcome aboard, Amy. Is Sara in?"

"No, she called and said to give her another hour. The baby has a cold." Amy laughed. "Oh, the joys of motherhood; I can't wait. Oh yes, there's somebody to see you."

Casey? She felt her heart flip. Impossible.

"A kid, she's about fifteen. She's in the ladies' room right now. Looks as if she's been crying."

"Oh dear." Julie sighed. Since the program a couple of weeks before on Halloran House, a home in Manhattan for runaways, two or three kids had dropped by each week to see her. "Amazing how people find their way here," she said.

"It's a cold world out there," Amy said. She reached for a batch of messages and handed them to Julie. "Your voice sounds so warm on the air, they think you have the answer to all their problems."

"Look," Julie said, spontaneously deciding not simply to pass on the literature she had available, "send her back to me when she comes out. I started the whole thing by inviting Father Halloran to *Night Talk*. I really ought to finish it."

She couldn't shake the sense of dejection she had felt all day and when she went into her office, she slammed the door behind her. Somehow the small space she had wanted to escape from earlier that evening now made her feel more in control. When she'd been a child and things had gotten out of hand, she used to race for the tiny bathroom she shared with her mother and sister, lock the door, and stay there reading. She supposed she had never gotten rid of the habit of going into hiding when life got rough.

She was gazing idly at her messages when the intercom buzzed. Her immediate thoughts went to Casey and she took a deep breath before picking up the receiver.

"I'm sending her back." It was Amy at the reception desk.

"Who?" Julie asked before she heard the disconnection. The teenager in tears, she supposed. She waited, still feeling the same emptiness, until a soft knock sounded at the door.

"Come in."

The door opened slowly and her niece Lindy peered in. "Aunt Julie?"

Julie was up and around her desk, taking her niece in her arms at once. "Well, for heaven's sake, what are you doing here?'' She noted first the red-rimmed eyes and then the overnight case that Lindy carried. "Hey honey, what's the matter? What's wrong?''

The tears started and Lindy allowed herself to be drawn over to a chair.

"Lindy, what's wrong?'' Julie squatted on her haunches and tilted her niece's chin. "Does your mom know you're here?''

Lindy shook her head, and then turned pleading eyes to Julie. "Oh, please don't tell her.''

"Hey, come on,'' Julie began cheerfully. "Let's wipe those tears. I'll get you something to drink from the soda machine and then we can sit down and talk. How's that? It can't be too bad, can it?''

Lindy looked at her and shook her head in a gesture that Julie couldn't interpret. She picked up a couple of tissues and dabbed carefully at her niece's eyes. "What I like,'' she said, "is a beautiful young girl who doesn't wear a smidgen of makeup on her eyes.'' She was talking just to say things. "Now, wait one minute and I'll get you that soda.''

As she raced down the corridor a hundred questions crossed her mind, but Julie decided it was probably nothing more than a spat with her mother. She would have to call Bobbie, and for a moment thought of doing so out of Lindy's hearing, but realized it wouldn't be fair. Lindy had come to her for help and the least she could do was hear her out. When Julie came back with the soda, she was thankful to see that Lindy had been sitting quietly waiting for her, dry-eyed. She reached gratefully for the drink.

Julie pulled her chair around and then grasped her niece's hand. "Want to tell me about it?''

Lindy took in a deep gulp. "He hits me,'' she said in a low voice.

Julie felt a slow dread spread through her and she closed her eyes to stem the feeling of nausea. "Who?" Yet she knew beforehand what the answer would be.

"Dan."

"What do you mean, he hits you?"

"Well, you know. He got mad because I was playing some music too loud and he told me to stop and I didn't."

"Why didn't you turn it off or at least turn it down?"

"'Cause you can't listen to music low," Lindy said impatiently.

"Did he actually hit you for that?"

"Well, not exactly," Lindy said, coloring and backtracking, "but he wanted to. I saw that he was clenching his fist and he's not my father and he has no right to tell me what to do." Lindy looked at her with imploring eyes.

"But he didn't actually strike you, Lindy, did he?" Julie stroked her niece's hair. She remembered Casey's observations on Dan at her sister's party.

"Dan doesn't like me," Lindy said, with a catch in her voice. "He tries to hide it, but I know. He thinks I'm in the way."

"Lindy, you're wrong. He married your mother and took you on as his daughter. I know he cares deeply about you. It's just that he's feeling enormous pressure on the job. He's, well, he's in a little trouble now."

"What kind of trouble?" Lindy looked at her out of round, questioning eyes.

"Your mother has to discuss it with you."

"No! Please don't call her, Aunt Julie. I came to stay with you. She'd blame me, I know she would." The tears began to fall relentlessly. "You don't want me here, no one does."

Julie put her arm around her. "You know, your mother is my big sister and when I was a teenager I always used to go to her with my problems and she always understood."

"Really?"

"Girl Scouts honor."

Lindy gave her a tearful, relieved smile as Julie picked up the receiver.

Her sister answered on the first ring. From the sound of her voice, Julie knew how upset she was. "Take it easy, Bobbie," she said at once. "I have Lindy here with me. It's all a tempest in a teapot. I'm going to put her on the phone. She has something to say to you."

She handed the receiver to her niece and listened quietly. When her niece hung up, Julie came over and wrapped her arms around her.

"She's coming to get me," Lindy said.

"Will you be all right?"

Lindy shook her head. "I guess you think I'm an awful brat. I love you, Aunt Julie."

"I love you too, Lindy. If you need me anytime, day or night, just call. Promise?"

Lindy hugged her. "I promise."

There was something else on Julie's mind, as she held her niece tightly. Kids in trouble—some a lot deeper than Lindy. Kids with no place to go—no aunts to sort things out with. If there had been no Julie, the alternative to Lindy's problems might have been the streets. It occurred to her as she gave her niece a final squeeze that there was a program idea in it, and she knew just the man to call.

Eight

Julie, who had kept from Sara all mention of Casey and her feelings about him, blurted out Lindy's problems at once as soon as Sara stepped into the office.

"Where is she?" Sara asked.

"I told her to go into the music library where she can play all those lovely rock tapes until Bobbie shows up. After all, it's her kind of music, isn't it?" Julie hesitated, picking up a paper clip and bending it apart. "Sara, would you think I'm cold and calculating if I tell you what's on my mind?"

"You want to do a show about Lindy?"

"You're close, but that's a little too close," Julie said carefully, throwing the paper clip on the desk. "That program we did on Father Halloran and Halloran House brought a number of sad, lost kids into his fold. I'm thinking of something more ambitious than that one. He was only part of a two-hour dialogue with representatives

of various services that were available for the disfran-
chised. How about..." she paused, took in a deep breath
and smiled. "A week-long series devoted solely to the
problem of runaways?"

Sara sifted through some material on her desk. "I was
sitting here wondering what will happen to my daughter
when she's in her terrible teens. You think you're doing
everything right..." She let the thought fade away.

"That's what I mean," Julie said. "This time we'll have
the runaways themselves on. Maybe some parents, psychologists, Father Halloran again, social workers, the
whole gamut. But mainly the kids. Kids every night, talking, explaining, letting all the terribleness out." She felt the
excitement grow, especially when Sara's expression grew
from skepticism to enthusiasm.

"When do you plan this event?"

"Three weeks from now, a month?" Julie shrugged.
She'd want the full services of both the publicity and promotion departments.

"Better make it a month," Sara said. "Problems, followed by various methods of solution. It could generate
some real interest."

Julie wondered what Casey would think of the program. She felt a sudden, almost touchable longing to find
him wherever he was and tell him everything. He'd picked
up on the tension in her sister's household, though Julie
had believed it was merely a ruse at the time to get her away
from the party. She hadn't forgotten his words, however.
She had thought long and hard about her brother-in-law's
problems. Because of that she had been able to act quickly
and decisively and she wanted Casey to know.

"I've a stake in this one," Julie told Sara simply.

That night sleep came hard. Then, when at last she slept, her dreams were of Casey making love to her, a Casey of surprising sweetness. In her dream she knew him, knew the way his body moved, knew the beat of his heart, the feel of his breath against her skin. In her dream, she reached out for him only to have him pull away suddenly. She wakened, in the middle of the night, perspiration covering her body, a flush on her face. She got up and went into the shower and stood under it, letting the warm rivulets run down her face and over her body.

One long week without hearing from Casey and it seemed like forever. "Call, damn you," she said out loud when she came back into her bedroom. She gave the telephone a murderous glance, as though it were at fault. And if he did call, what then? She would be obliged to argue with him over something, everything, nothing. It was a way of life between them.

She was toweling her hair dry when the telephone suddenly rang, its sound a lonely, mournful cry. She froze. Sara? No, Sara would be safely asleep in her husband's arms. Certainly not her sister, although she could never keep Julie's working hours straight. She went into her bedroom and sat down on the bed, counting the rings. On the fourth, she reached for the receiver and put it carefully to her ear. "Yes?"

"Don't hang up" were his first words.

She waited a long moment before answering, knowing the pounding in her heart wouldn't stop. "Give me one good reason not to."

"Because I don't want you to."

She heard the pleading in his tone and couldn't resist the thrust. "And what Casey wants, Casey gets." They were at it again. Fear of getting hurt, she supposed the psychologists would dub it.

"Not always," he was saying. "In fact, something I wanted very much slipped through my fingers."

"You'll get over it. It was a learning experience."

"I keep thinking there's something I'm supposed to apologize about," he said softly. "So I'd like to apologize."

"Casey," she began and then stopped.

"Go on."

"Where are you calling from?"

"Dallas. There's an hour's time difference. What are you doing right now?"

"Drying my hair." She imagined him in a lavish hotel room, lying on a king-sized bed, phone in his hand while the television set, the sound turned low, replayed some old movie.

"Then to sleep?" he asked.

"I thought of making some scrambled eggs."

"I've spent the week thinking about you," he said. " found it a little hard to concentrate on my work."

"Exactly what work are you doing, Casey?"

There was a long pause before he answered. She thought perhaps they had been disconnected. "Scouting sites for Graff Corporation."

She felt a long, cold draining. "They mean to stay in the radio business, then."

He laughed. "You got me. I'm only doing the foot work. Julie," he went on, his voice never more serious, " didn't call you to talk about work. I called because wanted to hear your voice."

"Here it is then. I'm still not quite certain I can believe that's all you want, even a thousand miles away."

"Damn it," he said, "I'm trying to touch you. Let me get close."

"I can't, Casey. You have the power to hurt me and I can't take the chance."

He was silent, although she could hear his soft, steady breathing. "I won't hurt you, Julie." The words were gently spoken and she sensed the longing in them that matched her own.

"Casey, let me go."

"I can't."

"Why? Am I some kind of challenge?"

"If I were with you," he said, "I'd be able to tell you, but there's a thousand cold miles between us and all I know is that I want to be with you. I want to hold you again. I want to bolt all the doors so that you can't run away."

The words were the sweetest she had ever heard and she felt the tears start to her eyes. "Don't," she whispered.

"What are you wearing right now, right this minute?"

She breathed a sigh of relief. He was going to keep it light, not bring back the moment when they'd been locked tight in one another's arms. If he did, she knew she couldn't bear it. "What am I wearing? A granny nightgown, with a bright-yellow towel around my head. Very staid."

"Granny nightgown. I'll have to do a little heavy shopping tomorrow. Something red and silky is how I pictured it."

"What are *you* wearing, Casey?"

He laughed. "What I always wear, my natural skin. Julie," he went on in a low tone, "tell me what I want to hear. That you think about me, you want to feel me in your arms, that you want me."

"In that order?"

"Be serious. In any order. Tell me."

"What do you really want to hear, Casey? I'm not sure."

"Of course you are." There was a long, connected silence between them in which perhaps more was said than by any words either might have spoken. "I'm going to have to eat crow; is that it?" he asked at last.

"About what?" Her words sounded braver than she meant. "I can't imagine what you'd be eating crow about."

"We're dancing around the subject. My feelings about you, your feelings about me. But maybe you're right. Maybe long-distance isn't the way to do it."

She realized he was making love to her despite her unreceptiveness, but she couldn't accept it. She didn't want his arms around her even figuratively, not now, not quite yet. "When will you be back in New York, Casey?" she asked as though it were round one in the bout to get him to hang up.

"According to my schedule, another week."

Another week. She thought—with an ache in her heart—that the time had never seemed so far away. "Well, if you're as busy as I am, then it should fly by."

"All the debris of our lives will have been cleared away by then," he said. "It'll be just Julie and Casey starting afresh."

She closed her eyes and gripped the receiver tightly, pressing it so hard against her ear that she felt a low throbbing. She didn't want him to say the words although they seemed to hum along the wire. "Goodbye, Casey. I've really got to get some sleep. I'll talk to you tomorrow," she said quickly and put down the receiver. *I love you.* The words might have come out of their own accord and she wasn't ready for them.

The next afternoon after a jaunty walk downtown from her apartment, Julie made her first stop in the publicity department of WRBZ.

"Dale in?" she asked the secretary to the publicity chief.

The response she got was a little disconcerting. It had been a rhetorical question. The door to Dale's inner office was partially open and she heard his booming voice from beyond.

"Let me check." His secretary paused, looked back at the door and then jumped up and ran into the office, closing the door behind her.

When she came back, his secretary gave her an abashed smile. "He's off the phone now," she said. "Go on in."

Well, well, well, thought Julie. The big man is apparently getting bigger by the minute.

Dale was at his desk, leaning across it, extending his hand before she even closed the door. "Hey, good to see you," he said. "Have a seat and some coffee, maybe?" He waited for Julie to sit down and then took his seat. The office was a large, airy one, fit for the head of publicity and promotion for the station. Attractive posters lined the walls, extolling the virtues of an all-rock station. There was no sign anywhere that he was also responsible for Julie's show.

She spoke up at once. "No coffee, Dale. I'll just be a minute. It's about my upcoming show on runaways. I sent you a memo. I wondered if you've worked out anything yet in the way of publicity. We've only got three weeks left."

"Yeah, right, I read the memo." He got to his feet, and turned briefly to the window and the view it commanded of the city. "Great concept." Then he turned back to her and said swiftly, "Look, kid, I'm sorry, but I have orders and a budget to stick to. Every damn cent is going to plug the station and music." He shrugged and sat down, reaching into a box for a cigar. She thought without the least amusement that he had probably taken to cigars because of Norbert Graff.

"Some phone calls and a couple of news releases can't break the station," she said quietly.

He leaned back in his chair, swiveling it to the right while he lit the cigar. "Julie, I can't."

She got hotly to her feet. "What are you trying to tell me?" she asked. "Is it Casey Phillips? Did he send the word down that *Night Talk* is off-limits to the publicity department?"

"Hey, come on, take it easy," he said, looking nervously at her.

"Dale," she said carefully, coming over to his desk and leaning on it with her hands, "we've known each other a long time now. We've even had a drink or two after hours. I really hate to see you treating me as if you've just discovered I've got a terrible disease. You got the word from Casey Phillips to lay off *Night Talk*, didn't you?"

"Julie, it's my job to take orders. If I could I'd give your program top priority, you know that."

"Just out of curiosity," she said, "when did that order come down the pike? I mean, Casey's been out of town for a week now."

"Look, kid," he said soothingly, "if it's any consolation, it came in with a bigger signature on it than Casey's."

She straightened up. "Norbert Graff." She turned and went over to his door. "See you, Dale. Don't lose any sleep over it."

The signature might be Norbert Graff's, she thought, but the budget was Casey's bailiwick. That was one of the things they had hired him for, wasn't it? Well, there were lots of ways to skin the publicity cat. She would handle it herself—and of course, there was always Drew. As for Casey, soft words and a hard heart. Well, there would be nothing harder than her resolve, if and when he called again.

"I'll get it," she said to Sara as she came into her office and heard the phone ringing. "Julie Garrett, *Night Talk*."

"What do you say to a twice-weekly segment on Channel Eight's *Anything Goes*, Julie my girl?" It was the excited voice of her agent, Maurie Smith.

For a moment her disappointment once again that it wasn't Casey sat there, impeding the full meaning of the words.

"I said," Maurie began again.

"Wait, I heard you, I heard you." She mouthed the words, "my agent," to Sara, sitting across the desk. "I just don't believe it."

"You know the program," Maurie was saying. "I told them the evening doesn't begin for you unless you watch it."

"Oh absolutely, I'm a slave to it, an absolute slave." Julie narrowed her eyes, trying to visualize the program called *Anything Goes*. "I've seen it dozens of times," she lied gamely, knowing Maurie wouldn't believe a word of it. "Every night, a half hour after the seven o'clock news." It was called the "Magazine of the Air," and like a magazine, had longer special features and short segments that dealt with health, food, the law. Where, she wondered, could she possibly fit in?

"Just five minutes each time for which you'll be paid the lordly sum of... whatever we arrive at in due time. Something in the nature of half the national budget. Say no, Julie Garrett, and I'll draw out a contract on you."

"Wait a minute," Julie said, "Let me catch my breath. All this just out of the blue, without interviews? Something's fishy, Maurie. You're springing this on me."

"Not springing, Julie. Just an intelligent decision in times of stress. No use getting your hopes up only to have them dashed at the last minute," Maurie told her in a very practical manner. "We've actually got something here, which is why I've called you. I played them your tapes. They've heard your program and interviews will be set up, all in due time; don't rush them. We're discussing the higher reaches of fame and fortune here, and they know what they want. You don't personally interview the presidential candidate before you pull the lever in the voting booth. You just add up the facts, ma'am. You, apparently, might just fill the ticket if you behave yourself and eat your porridge like a good girl."

"Maurie, I love what you're saying, but you're moving too fast," Julie told him, feeling as though the office had suddenly emptied of air and she had to gasp for breath. Then she added, "It's too sudden."

"What do you mean?"

"I don't know. I've still my contract to fulfill at the station."

"There's nothing wrong with crossover, as far as they're concerned. As a matter of fact, they'll only go with a winner."

"A winner," Julie echoed. She felt as if she were becoming dumber by the minute.

"You'll be given your own ticket on this one, and a staff. Come up with two stories a week—human interest stuff, back-to-basics stuff—and it's all in the hopper, ready to roll. There won't be any conflict with WRBZ. You won't be appearing live on screen, so you can budget your time to suit yourself."

"Oh be still, my beating heart," Julie said, feeling the first waves of excitement roll over her, and wondering why she had been holding back. "This will make all the difference, won't it?"

"You mean you can tell WRBZ where to go? What's his name, Casey Phillips?"

"No," she said, firmly. "That's not what I mean."

But Maurie always shied away from his clients' personal affairs, and didn't even try to follow up her remark. "Well, I'll keep you informed, kid. Just start thinking up what you have in store for them and make it look good."

"Visions of sugarplums are already dancing in my head." When she hung up, she sat for a long time staring at Sara with a silly look on her face.

"I looked that way when the doctor told me I was pregnant," Sara said at last. "What's your excuse?"

"Fame and fortune. We're talking megabucks here," Julie said, imitating Maurie's voice. "We're talking Channel Eight and *Anything Goes*—the program, that is."

"Oh, Julie, fantastic," Sara said, her eyes wide and bright with a happiness that held only goodwill. "What is it? Tell me everything from the beginning."

There was no beginning, Julie thought. Only a sudden about-face and a sharp right turn. This was one time she wouldn't come smack up against Casey Phillips.

"Would you take it?" Sara asked.

Julie told her about her meeting with Dale. "They're really putting me on the back burner. I don't have any choice. But I'm not going to jump the gun. I've got to have the interview with Channel Eight first."

It was nearly 6:00 P.M. when her agent called back. "Tomorrow morning," he said at once. "Ten o'clock. If you'll present yourself at the offices of Channel Eight, a certain Mr. Lane would like to see you."

"Tomorrow," Julie groaned. "What do you mean? I thought I'd have a little time."

"You do, all night."

"Thanks ever so much, Maurie. I'd better hang up now so that I can go bang my head against the wall."

"Listen, Julie, love, I also found out who your competition is."

"Don't tell me," she said. "Let me guess. The station manager's niece."

"Close," Maurice said. "She's a distant relation of the show's producer, but the trouble is her credentials are right up to the mark. She's in Philadelphia and professional right down to her toes. Also good-looking. Never hurts to know your competition is just that."

"I guess," Julie said slowly, feeling the most acute disappointment, "that I shouldn't lose any sleep over the interview, then."

"On the contrary. They like you, they know what you can do, and after that it's in the hands of the wee folk. I'll stop by the station later tonight and we can talk about it. How's that?"

"You're an angel, Maurie," Julie said, genuinely grateful. "Maybe it's better if the whole thing comes out of the blue like that. I'll have no time to think or worry or plan ahead."

"Ciao."

The offices of Channel Eight were downtown on the West Side, near the water. Development of the area had been slow to take place, but now, as in most parts of the city, signs of gentrification were everywhere. Small manufacturing buildings had been turned into condominiums; side streets of aging brownstones were being razed for purposes not clearly stated, or had been remodeled into expensive housing.

There were no parks, and as she stepped out of the cab in front of the nondescript eight-story building in which the television station was housed, she thought this might be a good program idea. Gentrification, without trees. Waiting for the elevator, she took a quick look at herself in her compact mirror. She was wearing a gray print silk dress under a black linen jacket and looked a professional all the way down to her pointed black shoes.

The producer of *Anything Goes* was a tall, slender man with a narrow, handsome face and gray hair, dressed in jeans and a blue denim shirt. Somehow she had expected to be greeted by a station committee all lined up, but he was alone in his office.

He gave her an admiring glance as his secretary ushered her into his office. How like Casey Phillips, she thought. Casual, yet sending off signals of success like Morse code messages. After asking Julie to take a seat in his messy, antique-filled office, he leaned back in his chair and put his feet on the desk.

"Well," he said in a deep, calm voice, "we've been very impressed with your tapes, and the program itself."

"Thank you," she said brightly, tipping her head and smiling at him. She had become calm as soon as the effects of Maurie's telephone call had worn off, adopting an attitude of insouciance. It never paid to worry when relatives of program producers were your competition.

"We want somebody bright, sassy, a reporter of odd little facts about city life. As you know, *Anything Goes* is syndicated, but has a local flavor. Everyone is fascinated with New York," he said, "even though nobody wants to live here."

"I wish you'd tell my landlord that the next time he asks for a rise in rent."

He smiled. "We figure that you know the city, and that you've got enough facts on file to take you through the year 2000. In other words, Julie, we like your style and what you have up here." He tapped his head with his finger. "The segments are five minutes apiece and they could cover anything from how fish is brought into the city, to ten ways to save money on taxes, provided it's visual and holds the viewer's attention."

"But nothing heavy," Julie put in.

He nodded. "Nothing heavy. Our listeners have heard it all on the seven o'clock news. Now they want us to say, 'Hey, it's okay. Here's where the fun is.'"

It was the one aspect of the program she could take exception to—only seeing the bright side of the city. She preferred to confront the more serious aspects of life, take on subjects that really meant something to people.

"I see a slight frown on your face," he threw in. "We don't mean it has to be a bundle of laughs. The city's a great cultural institution and we don't want you to stay away from controversial subjects as long as they don't give our viewers nightmares. The program *is* syndicated and may be viewed one day in New York and another in the West."

"I've been thinking a lot about it," Julie said. "And I've a number of ideas."

They talked for a while, interrupted by several telephone calls. "Well," he said, after fifteen minutes had gone by, straightening up, "I think you know what we want now. These are only preliminary talks. I'll look forward to seeing you again." He came around his desk and shook hands with her.

She gripped his hand with a strong, solemn shake. "Thank you for seeing me, and I'll look forward to talking to you again, also." It was only when she stepped outside that she allowed herself to think. The preliminaries. The producer has his quick impression, discovers I'm made of flesh and blood and I'm no closer than before.

Nine

Café Argenteuil was on a side street off Madison Avenue, and it was there, midway through the week, that Julie met Sheila Salisbury for lunch. She hadn't heard from her agent since her interview at Channel Eight, but she had deliberately pushed it to the back of her mind. They knew what they wanted, and she either fitted the bill or didn't. There was no use worrying about it. The best part of it was that she was being considered for the job. Meanwhile, there were more pressing problems, including the call from Sheila to meet her for lunch.

"What's happening?" were Julie's first words after she greeted the head of L.O.W.

"Much ado about everything," Sheila said as soon as they were seated in the tiny garden out back. The day was pleasantly cool, with dark clouds scooting down from the northwest and the scent of rain in the air. The distant sound of traffic and the soft murmur of voices in the garden added a discreet enchantment to the noon hour. Like Paris, Julie thought as she settled back in an iron chair and took up the menu. Only in Paris, according to the script, you sat with the man you loved and held hands across the table.

Casey hadn't called again. He might have hitched a ride to the moon for all she knew of his whereabouts. She had rehearsed a dozen times over what she planned to say to him if he called, but he didn't. It was possible he knew just what had happened, and was staying away. The trouble was, Julie was hurt, and in love, and had no real idea how to handle it.

"We're still pulling in responses to the ad," Sheila said brightly, interrupting her reverie and looking at her with a curious smile. "About a thousand now. *And* money. Not bad. Drew," she added, "has even managed a plug in Suzy's column in the *Post*." She pulled the clipping out and quoted, "'Social Notes From All Over. Question: Will the best radio station in the metropolitan area go down the drain?' Lovely to make it into the most popular gossip column in the city."

Julie laughed, her attention revived. "I saw it. I hope Norbert Graff saw it, too. I slipped it to his secretary and she gave me a broad enough wink."

Sheila picked up the menu and then said across it, "The FCC has set a date for the hearing. We're going down to Washington en masse, and we want you to sit in as a 'friend' of L.O.W. Will that mean trouble chez WRBZ?"

The waiter came by and gave them an attentive nod. "Anything to drink, mesdames?"

"Wine?" Julie looked across at Sheila.

"White."

Their orders complete, Sheila went directly back to the subject that interested her most. "What about it? Will it make things tough for you if you come down with us?"

Julie, buttressed by the possibility of getting the job with Channel Eight, shook her head. "I can afford to be daring."

"Uh-oh, that sounds dangerous. Anything wrong at the station?"

"No." Julie toyed with the idea of telling Sheila about her interview, but decided against it. She marked it down to wanting to keep to the point, and Channel Eight was a digression. But there was something else, too—a vague superstition, the feeling that every day enlarged the bubble she was in, that the walls were growing thinner and thinner and would ultimately break if she weren't careful.

"Is it possible for you to come down with us, Julie? I know it's short notice, but suddenly the FCC wants to clear its calendar before summer. Anyway, these things shouldn't really drag on too long. If we count the calendar from the day L.O.W. was conceived by Eleanor and me, six months have gone by. The further away we get from the original programming, the less likely we'll be to get any semblance of it back. You, for instance," she said. "Somebody's bound to make you a great offer once you're on the market."

Julie laughed. "Line forms to the right."

"Incidentally," Sheila went on, "we're bringing down a couple of your old friends." She rattled off the names of a few of the people who had lost their jobs at WRBZ with the changeover in programming.

Julie whistled. "Of course I'll come, Sheila. The only problem is time. My program is five nights a week. I could repeat one, of course," she added thoughtfully, running quickly over past programs that might do for a repeat. A smile curled her lips. "My famous contract allows me time off here and there, and I never really take advantage of it. I also can rerun whatever program I want to."

"Lovely contract," Sheila said.

"I've got a good lawyer and a good agent."

"That's the way it should be," Sheila said, smiling, "although I would have loved having you as a client."

"I could rerun the L.O.W. program," Julia said slowly. "That would certainly be something."

Sheila continued to smile, but then spoke up, surprising Julie. "Norbert Graff is bragging that he's going to bury us. That's the scuttlebutt I've heard. It wouldn't make any sense to light that kind of fire under him, repeating the program, if he already warned you off."

"There's not too much they can do to me."

"If," Sheila went on, "we get what we want and WRBZ returns to its original format, you'll still have to deal with them. You're going on as if you'll be out of a job in a few months, no matter what."

Julie sighed. "I suppose it's the way I've been feeling and acting lately."

"Anything you want to talk about? I've a pretty big ear."

"No, I'm a little tired maybe," Julie said. "My biological clock always runs a little oddly because of the late-night show. But I'll tell you what I'm planning for *Night Talk*: Runaways." She stopped, noted the interested look in Sheila's eyes and wondered if she could use her expertise. She was never shy about using friends for charitable purposes.

"Go on," Sheila said gently.

"I'm involved with something right now, a really inter esting, newsworthy program that's taking up all my en ergy." She paused and then added, "I've got a kind o personal stake in how it turns out."

The waiter came with their wine. "I don't under stand," Sheila said, wrapping her fingers around the coo stem of her glass.

Julie quickly outlined the projected program. "I'd lik to hit you, Drew, everybody for help, but I don't dare," she added, "knowing how much you're all doing just t keep the station going."

"When is the program scheduled?"

"Week after next, but don't worry; not yet anyway. I'n just anticipating problems, and if anything happens, we' have you guys in our corner. As for Washington, of cours I'll come down. Will it take one day or more?"

Sheila shrugged. "As far as we can tell, no more than day, but we're not the only complainants being heard b the commissioners of the Mass Media Bureau. We'r bringing down a force of at least fifty interested observ ers. I imagine Graff will bring down that many lawyers."

"Tell me what you want me to do, and I'll be there," Julie said, feeling a certain sense of wonder that they ha accomplished so much so quickly. The game itself ha changed. The decision, after all, wouldn't come to whethe she was so good that Casey would have to keep her on, bu whether Graff would win or lose the battle to keep its li cense.

"You look a little worried," Sheila said.

"If Graff loses its license to operate WRBZ, it'll have t find a buyer," Julie said. "If it fails to find a buyer, the what?"

"It'll find a buyer," Sheila said with determination. "Radio stations are a very valuable commodity these days. Compared to television, they're relatively cheap to run, and they make lots of money. I'm not so certain Graff will give up the license so easily. One of the things we're all going to have to do," she said with a laugh, "is make certain we buy the products advertised on the station. I never thought I'd see the day when I'd be hawking advertising."

"It's the democracy we live in," Julie said, feeling unexpectedly solemn. "There are trade-offs of all kinds." She thought of how her program depended upon selling itself, selling advertising, even selling the people who tuned in.

"Are you all right?" Sheila's voice broke into her thoughts.

"I'm all right," Julie said. She raised her wineglass in a salute. "Here's to Washington and victory."

The capitol lay under gray, low-lying clouds, making the white government buildings look stark and dramatic against the background of the morning sky.

Julie, hurrying into the Federal Communications Building on M Street, noted almost absentmindedly that the building was certainly government issue, perhaps ten or fifteen years old, a monument neither to good nor to bad taste.

The hearing was being held in the eighth-floor boardroom and by the time she got there, it was already in session. The room was paneled in a warm, burnished wood, also government issue, she reflected. A flag stood in the right-hand corner. At the rear the seats for observers were filled to overflowing. At the front, wide oak desks faced the long dais at which the commissioners sat with their advisers.

Sheila and the others had come down the night before to powwow before the hearing took place. Julie, however, had taken an early morning flight. She'd reserved a flight back to New York, but asked Sara nonetheless to make a hotel reservation for her, just in case.

Sheila, who had obviously been looking for Julie, waved her to the seat next to her. Drew Berkeley was there, along with Eleanor Stein, Bill MacDonald and half a dozen people who had worked at WRBZ. She also noted the presence of a few New York journalists representing the arts and entertainment sections of various popular magazines and newspapers. It might seem to be a local fight, but it had national implications. Of course, the interest and coverage might be after the fact. Once the case was presented to the commissioners of the FCC's Mass Media Bureau, it would be all over but the waiting. She didn't suppose for a minute that decisions were made on the basis of how the popular press reported a story.

"I was right about the heavies Graff brought down," Sheila whispered. She named the principals of one of New York's most prestigious law firms who sat a few feet away. Norbert Graff was there, deep in consultation with someone Julie didn't recognize. She realized that her heart had been pounding since she had first stepped off the elevator onto the eighth floor. She had somehow expected to see Casey but a quick glance around the room showed he wasn't there.

"We're next on the agenda," Sheila told her. "The group they're hearing from now has a similar problem in Oregon and it'll be interesting to learn how they've handled it."

It was just before noon when the case of "Listeners of WRBZ" against the Graff Corporation was finally taken up.

The commissioner, after looking at his notes for a while, consulted his watch. "I think we'll take a break about now for lunch, and start the proceedings again at two o'clock."

Julie heard Sheila's clear groan in the general noise and shuffling that erupted at once. "We'll never get through this day," she said. "I'll bet it'll be dragged over until tomorrow."

"I can stick it out if you can," Julie said.

They had lunch in a small, nondescript restaurant nearby. No one felt much like eating and the discussion kept to the issues. Julie was surprised at how relaxed she had become. It was like waiting for an operation. At the moment she was completely anesthetized.

The hearing began promptly at two. The room was still packed, although many faces had changed. She still didn't see Casey and found herself turning at each little sound, searching the room for him. Now they sat at the front, at the big oak tables recently abandoned by the group from Oregon.

Sheila insisted that Julie stay with her. "There are few enough of you left at WRBZ. I want you here where the commissioners can get a good look at you."

"So will Norbert Graff," Julie said dryly.

Drew sat on her other side, and before the meeting was called to order, he whispered into her ear. "I thought they'd bring on Casey Phillips."

"Who knows?" she remarked lightly. "He might come in at the last minute on a white charger. He'd do that sort of thing."

Drew leaned back. "He can swing in through the window like Tarzan. The commission has made a number of decisions pro cases like ours. It'll be a pleasure to see these guys knocked out of the ring."

The case for L.O.W. was given quickly and succinctly by
Sheila, and was followed by Graff's presentation. The
commissioners and aides asked questions. Anything,
thought Julie as the hour wore on, was possible; everything sounded right from everybody's point of view. She
was a little drowsy. The sun came out and a shaft of light
through the window made the room suddenly warm.

It was three-thirty when there was a slight rustle at the
back. Julie, engaged in drawing doodles on the yellow-
lined pad before her, realized that she didn't dare turn
around. He had come into the hearing room, she was absolutely certain of it, as though he had been borne along
on his own airstream.

It was Graff's lawyer who confirmed it. "If the commission will give permission, our station manager has just
come in from a meeting in Chicago. He'd like to read a
statement, if he may."

Casey Phillips, white charger and all. She knew it. Julie
noted that the long, ragged line she drew tore right through
the paper. Sheila gently touched her arm. "Nothing like a
dramatic last-minute entrance," she said in a low voice.
"The big, handsome movie star come to save the station
from being sold down the river."

Julie laughed but wouldn't look up. She felt rather than
saw him take a seat in the Graff camp to her left. She was
drained of all energy, afraid somehow that his arrival signaled disaster.

Drew Berkeley leaned over and whispered in her ear.
"You know who came in with him? Senator Glidden, of
the financial appropriations committee. Looks like our
man has friends in the right places."

"Gentlemen," Casey began, his voice never more
warmly attractive, "when I was hired by the Graff Corporation to turn WRBZ into a profitable operation, I was

ompletely conversant with the tenets of broadcasting ac-
ording to FCC rules: a station is meant to serve its lis-
ners." He paused, then repeated the sentence: "A station
s meant to serve its listeners. A simple enough phrase."

Julie, by leaning forward slightly, found he had taken a
eat on Graff's right side, which placed him in her line of
ight. Wearing a blue suit with his tie neatly knotted, here
vas Casey in a role she had never expected him to play.

As though he knew she was there, he turned toward her,
lso leaning forward a little, his eyes settling on her for a
rief moment before he looked away. "We all agree to
hat," he went on. "Serving our listeners is the operative
dea. Yet every survey we've taken indicates the numbers
or retaining the old programming aren't there. The lis-
eners of the old WRBZ have never bothered making
hemselves heard before. As for their numbers..." He
topped, letting the laugh in his voice finish the sentence
or him.

"Demographics," Sheila said in an aside to Julie. "If I
ear that word once more—"

"He hasn't said it yet," Julie pointed out, but she didn't
eel like laughing.

"He will," Sheila said.

But he didn't. Speaking in slow, well thought-out cad-
nces, the man in the dark suit was someone Julie didn't
ecognize. He no longer was the laid-back boss of a radio
tation, but a hard-nosed businessman with pages of red
nk to wash out, an injured businessman trying to pay off
is stockholders. He didn't mention the word demo-
raphics once.

"A handful of people tuning in as if the airwaves were
heir own private preserve," he went on, "are just a small
egment of a community we've been given a mandate to
erve. Where are the rest, may I ask? Dial-twisting adults

under thirty-five waiting in the wings for stations such a
WRBZ to ante up the kind of music they want, the kind o
programming they want. This group is waiting for a break
too. Aren't we committed to serving them, or do we con
tinue to go after a handful of people who can find othe
stations dishing up their kind of 'soul food'?"

Julie heard Sheila's audible but admiring sigh over hi
words. "Oh, hitting below the belt," she said. "I'll hav
to take him on, Julie, and forget the kid gloves."

"He's definitely not a kid gloves man," Julie re
marked. "He really believes all that junk he's saying. Thi
minute, anyhow."

"Advertisers flocked back with the change in program
ming," he was saying. "While we understand we're not i
business solely for the business of our advertisers, we nee
them and there's no pretending we don't. Improve
equipment, new studios, all those things that keep us up
to-date with our competitors, cost money.

"With deregulation, there's a good chance that WRB2
could and should win its right to operate as a rock station
However, Graff Corporation is willing to discuss certai
concessions on programming," he stated casually, th
words almost slipping by Julie.

"Classical and rock?" Drew said softly. "That's lik
putting mustard on a jelly sandwich."

"Somewhere someone likes jelly and mustard," Juli
threw in.

There was a murmur in the room and the commissione
looked as if he were about to call for attention when Ca
sey went on. "We have a late-night jazz program, *Coope*
on Jazz. We think there's a new crossover audience—or,"
he added, "if there isn't, there should be."

Julie felt a surge of happiness for Coop. His job wa
probably safe then. Sheila touched her wrist lightly. "Well

well, well," she said under her breath. "With that he's making things more difficult for us."

"*Night Talk*," Casey was saying. "A late-night talk, call-in show covering a variety of topics, local and national, some deadly serious, others..." He paused, but Julie merely looked straight ahead at the commissioners of the Mass Media Bureau who faced her. "Others," he said, "ephemera."

Sheila held tightly onto Julie's arm. He needs somebody to put on the rack, Julie thought, stunned, and he's using me. In the silence of the room, she heard the creak of a chair and sensed that he had leaned back in it in his characteristic way, wanting to loosen his tie and get comfortable.

"Tune into any late-night station and we find the same subjects being treated, over and over again. The only one making a profit is the telephone company. Yes, we think the under thirty-fives need a platform," he went on, "but one that's less ego-filled, that doesn't rely on the same few call-ins wanting to air the same old griefs. We'd like to open up the air late at night, have it less claustrophobic."

But Julie had stopped listening and sat there quietly, her hands in her lap, aware of nothing but the drumming of her heart.

Room 607. Just down the hall and to her left. It had taken a quick telephone call to New York to locate him. He was staying at the same hotel as she, convenient all around.

He could throw her out. He could call the house detective. He could fire her on the spot, but Casey Phillips would know exactly how she felt about him.

Forget the past, she told herself. The lovemaking, the soft words when he knew he had caught her. It had been a mistake she would have to live with.

Room 607. It popped up in front of her and Julie gave herself no time for further reflection, but pounded on the door. Raise the devil, for he was certainly that. She had no doubt he was there. She had made certain of that, too, with a discreet telephone call to the lobby.

The door opened suddenly, just as she lifted her hand again. He hadn't even bothered to inquire who was there.

"What took you so long?" he asked with a lazy smile that didn't quite reach his eyes.

"You son of a bitch," she said through gritted teeth.

"Well, good-humored, as usual," he said, throwing back his head and laughing. The sound was all she needed. Julie raised her hand to slap him but he caught her wrist and pulled her into the room.

"Now, now, a temper tantrum in the corridor will only bring the management." He propelled her forward, closing the door with a resounding bang.

"Take your hands off me." She felt her voice deadly calm.

"Only protecting myself," he said, the grin still on his face. "It seems to me that you're ready for an assault without a deadly weapon, but deadly nonetheless."

"Damn right." She pulled her hand away. "You won't get away with it."

"With what? I'm clean, so help me."

"Marching into the hearing with all those important papers, to say nothing of an array of blue-suited artillery from the legal department, pretending you're really serious about L.O.W."

"Pretending? Lady, you've got a redwood-sized chip on your shoulder."

"Your presentation was brilliant, right down to the last detail—that last detail being the insignificance of my show."

"You weren't listening," he said. "Oddly enough, my solipsistic friend, *Night Talk* isn't the only program on WRBZ. Naturally I went for the jugular, not only yours but everybody's. With the exception of Coop, of course."

"Well, thank goodness for small favors. You zeroed in on my show. Everyone got the picture." She was aware of him gazing at her as though he had conjured her up and was glad of what he saw. "And don't look at me like that," she added. "It won't work."

"Well, I knew you were in a snit when you walked out after the hearing was over, head held high." He leaned back against the mahogany dresser, his hands dug into his pockets. "But the truth is, I didn't expect you to run all the way here for a showdown. I had something else in mind."

"Oh, I ran all the way, Casey," she said. "I just wanted you to know how I admired your monumental genius. Coming into the meeting room with Senator Glidden was a master stroke. The commissioners must be shaking in their boots, since the Senator sits on the appropriations committee and is responsible for funding the FCC. Drew Berkeley thought he'd hand a little something in to the papers, just in case the reporters didn't catch the significance of it all. No doubt you were promising him something for his campaign chest next year? For favors granted, of course."

Something flared for an instant at the back of his eyes but was gone as quickly as it had come. "That's what you've come about," he said, more as a question than a statement. "Lady, you're about as wrong as you can be. I wonder why I bother with you."

The comment shocked her for a long moment, until she realized that he had put her on the defensive with his usual skill. "I never asked you to *bother* with me," she stated.

"You should've asked me about the senator first, instead of accusing me of doing something underhanded. I would have told you the truth. I've never lied to you."

"I wouldn't believe anything you said to me if you stood at the corner of Forty-second Street and Fifth Avenue and shouted it with a bullhorn."

He shook his head slowly, eyes narrowing as he regarded her intently. "The thought saddens me that I seem to have lost you somewhere."

"Along with your credibility."

"Julie, I don't want to lose you; I feel this whole thing is getting out of hand."

She was taken aback by his admission but still went doggedly on, knowing she hadn't told him all she wanted to. "You bet it's getting out of hand," she said. "That display of fireworks and pyrotechnics you put on for the committee taught me one thing: Find Casey Phillips's vulnerable spot and go for it."

He straightened and moved toward her, fists clenched and eyes blazing. "Damn the FCC and WRBZ and L.O.W. Damn this whole thing altogether. I'm tired of it. I did what I had to do, and that's the end of it. There's not a thing you could have said that would have made me change my mind." He reached out and grasped her arms. "Julie, you're my lover." As she caught her breath, he drew her close, ignoring the sudden stiffening of her body. "If you felt nothing for me, you wouldn't have come storming in here. You would have left the Senator Glidden foolishness to the committee, sued me in the courts, done anything but faced me down in my hotel room."

"You have it all wrong," she murmured and yet it seemed to her that however much she might resist, she couldn't move from the circle of his arms. "I thought, oh,'' she said with a deep sigh, ''I don't know what I thought.''

He released her and then taking up her hands, pressed his lips to each palm, the touch of his lips pulling a long wave of sensuality through her body. ''You're full of anger over one thing only,'' he said. ''Coming to my bed didn't quite get you what you thought it would.''

She gasped, stepping back. Withdrawing her hands from his, she automatically reached for a small book that lay on the bed table.

''You're not going to throw that,'' he said, looking at her askance.

''No,'' she said, putting the book down carefully. ''I'm going to do something far cleverer than that. I'm going to walk out of here and never see you again.''

''You're going to listen to me,'' he said, walking swiftly over to the door and leaning against it. ''You've been trying to tie the two together ever since we first met—your job and the fact that I was interested in you.''

''You fool, you're telling me that I slept with you just to keep my job,'' she stated indignantly, first clenching, then releasing her fists.

''I'd hate to think it wasn't my boyish charm and native good looks.''

Julie could feel the blood rush to her face. ''I hate you,'' she said in a cold, clear, precise manner. She went for him, raising her arms and pounding on his chest.

He grabbed both her wrists, holding them tightly, and pulled her close. ''Oh no, you don't,'' he said, breathing the words close to her lips. ''I've had just about enough.''

He picked her up, not at all gently, and swung her over his shoulder. Julie kicked, but he placed a restraining hand over her legs and carried her across the room where they landed in a tangle of limbs on the bed.

Julie squirmed out from under him and was about to rush off with what dignity she could muster when she made the mistake of looking back at Casey and losing herself in his smiling, hopeful eyes. She smiled, then began to laugh. "Oh, Casey, what are we doing to one another?"

He reached for her. "Making love in the craziest way possible." He clutched her close and came down hard on her lips.

Then the feel of his warm body against hers sent her into a tailspin and she opened her lips to him, returning his kisses with equal heat. He was right. They had been making love from the moment she had walked into his room. She wanted him. She was almost dazed from wanting him.

He lifted his head and smiled down at her. "Julie, stop for a moment." His fingers skimmed through her curls. "You know what I want."

He was against her now, hard and demanding, as if by sheer force he would brush aside any further objections she might have. "I'm not letting you go," he whispered into her mouth. "You mean too much to me."

Julie, staggered by his words, allowed her body to go limp against him.

"I want you," he told her. "It's all I think about." His words came as a husky whisper in her ear. Then his mouth moved over hers with an unconcealed, almost desperate hunger. It was beyond anything Julie had experienced before; the need she now sensed in him hadn't been there that first time. This kiss had a deliberate, seductive quality—teasing, testing, trapping her.

"Casey," she managed to say, drawing her lips away from his, "this doesn't change anything, you know that."

His grip tightened around her, as if he didn't trust what she might do. "Forget all that nonsense. It means nothing. It's just you and me. We're shutting the rest of it out."

"Casey, please, oh, Casey." She breathed out the words, surprised at the ache in her voice.

He caught her face between rough, urgent fingers, holding her as he rained a line of scorching kisses across her mouth and down her neck. "It's too late." He raised his head, his face inches from hers. "It was too late the moment I met you. Can't you see that? Nothing else matters, not the beginning, the middle or the end. For you and me it's bound to come out only one way."

She held herself still against the onslaught of his words. Everything he said was true, but somehow overwhelming. It was as if she had walked into the enemy camp and surrendered before she'd fought the battle.

One strong hand now held her head as the other ranged the length of her body. Julie gasped as he invaded her mouth, his tongue surging between her teeth, seeking the warm, moist interior.

A thrill coursed through her body as she felt the hard tendons of his thighs, and the unmistakable need that was pushing against her hip. He was unrelenting in his assault, and her body tightened as she fought for air. His hand found her breast and her breath caught in her throat. She didn't try to stop him because she knew then she couldn't have, even if she'd wanted to.

"Julie." The name was wrenched from him as his kiss changed and the pressure of his mouth on hers eased as he ran his tongue along her lips. When he lifted his head to look at her he said in a voice she had never heard before, "Put your arms around me. Let me know you want me. Don't make me wait."

He caressed her as he spoke and she gave in to the aching shivers of doubt and need that swept through her. Her gaze traveled to his face. She felt herself trapped by his eyes, trapped by a force so fierce and elemental that she couldn't speak.

Without thinking, she wound her arms around his body. A strange smile played around his lips. He had won, and she had wanted him to.

It was all over. The doubt was gone. She knew now, as surely as he did, that they would make love. Now, in the room she had gone to on a very different errand. He wanted her, and she trembled as a primitive part of her thrilled to it. She was obeying his command and yet she felt as if she had willed it, had known all along that it would end this way.

He fumbled with the buttons of her blouse and she caught his fingers, bringing them to her lips. He watched, his breath coming faster, as she slowly undid the buttons, tossing the clinging silk to the floor. Then he began to kiss her greedily as he undid the lacy bra and flung it aside. Lifting his head, he gazed at her through narrowed lids, groaning her name as he reached for her. She touched his hair with tentative, shaking fingers as he ran his hand down her body. In a few breathless moments he had her clothes off and, with his eyes never leaving her face, tore at his own.

He was the dream all over again, she thought. Wide, bronzed shoulders, dark-blond hair across his chest, slim hips. He caught her up in his arms and hugged her tightly before lying down beside her, fully aroused. "See what you do to me?" he said, enveloping her once more in his arms.

"Casey, I—"

"Don't talk."

He kissed her slowly at first, gently teasing her, letting her know that he needed her response. When she clung to him, urging him on, he uttered a deep, husky growl and moved his body over hers. Julie strained against him, crushing her breasts to the hard wall of his chest, knowing that she was losing herself in an intoxicating dream.

She had lost the ability to think coherently; she wanted what he offered, an embrace that promised such passion it would erase time and fill her senses forever. He was touching her now with exquisite tenderness, slowly savoring every moment as his body rhythmically moved against her. She turned her head for a moment, unable to catch her breath.

"Look at me." He mumbled the words now. "I need to know what you're feeling."

She didn't answer, but lay waiting.

"Don't hide from me," he said softly as his mouth found a nipple. Deliberately he moved her legs apart with his knee, burying his face in her breasts as his hand slid gently, knowingly to the soft warmth between her legs.

Julie choked back a sense of helplessness. Her heart pounded in her chest and with a sigh that went through her, she spoke his name.

"I know, love, I know," he said, kissing her deeply, his tongue hungrily invading her mouth and holding her captive. Her body arched into his as an uncontrollable shiver sped through her. She heard his low groan of desire as he rained kisses on her face, her throat, her shoulders and then gently bit at the soft flesh, sending a wave of fiery tension galloping along her spine.

Julie gripped him, making small sounds that seemed to come from far away. When she cried out once more, he slid his hands down the length of her back, and pressed her hard into the bed, his body heavy over her.

"It's going to be all right," he said. "I love you," he murmured, the words so low that she barely heard them, but the absolute certainty came through, engulfing her with a sense of wonder and rising hunger.

He was drawing small erotic circles on the inside of her thighs as her nails began to bite into the flesh of his shoulders. Then she held her breath as she lowered her hand to reach for him. She felt his body go still with anticipation. When she encircled him, he moaned low in her ear and gave a long, shuddering sigh. He found her lips again and plunged deep, drinking her as if he were dying of thirst.

His arms were like a steel band around her, taut with expectation. Her hands fluttered over him as he lowered his head once more. With gentle tugs he sent a scorching bolt that rippled through her, and she cried out, a cry of longing she made no attempt to hide. His mouth was wet and hot as he closed it over the other rosy circle.

His hand was now at the small of her back, urging her hips against the hard tension in his.

"I'm hooked on you," he said. "This must be how an addict feels. I don't think I'll ever get enough of you."

Julie felt the now familiar quivering in her abdomen; she moaned as his mouth trailed down her body. She arched convulsively as he knelt between her open thighs. When he touched her with his lips, she held her breath, stunned by the wonder of it. With his tongue and fingers working a gentle magic, she could stand it no longer. She reached for his head, urging him up. He stroked her and she moved her legs together, capturing his hand. For what seemed an eternity Julie held still, never wanting it to end; reaching a selfishness that astounded her, she felt unable to do anything about it. It was as if she had surrendered her very being. She uttered his name, and he kissed her as he whispered, "Let it happen again, Julie. Just let go." She shuddered and he let his hand rest until the waves had retreated. He seemed to know everything she was feeling.

When she was quiet, he said, "I can't wait any longer," the words husky with passion. He put both hands under her hips and raised her to him. He entered her, slowly at first and then when she raised her body toward him he surged forward and brought her close in a clinging rush. Julie gasped as she accepted the unrelenting impact of his body. As he drove into her, she felt her world come apart and splinter into a thousand shimmering shards. A tiny sensation that had no name started somewhere within her and built to a tension that made her feel feverish. She tried to resist, but a delight, sweet and unknown, took possession of her as she thrashed about beneath him. Then she was still, not wanting him to move either, as wave after wave of pure sensation swept through her. He understood and held her tight as she felt it subside. It was only then that he unleashed his own passion, hoarsely whispering her name as he thrust deeply into her, and then uttering a fierce, masculine cry.

Julie felt his spasmodic shiver as he drove into her one last time, and then lay still, his weight a warm blanket of protection.

Ten

___

Julie lay quietly, fully awake, staring at the smooth white ceiling and the first shafts of daylight that played through the soft curtains. For the first time in her life, she belonged to someone. He had been so possessive in his lovemaking that she had no doubt he was staking a claim. Yet she knew she had to hold back. Dreams didn't come true just because you wished hard.

Casey's head was on her shoulder, and she could hear his even breathing. She moved slightly, wanting him to waken. "I'm not sleeping," he said, his breath warm against her skin.

"I thought I'd lost you there for a moment," she said, laughing.

"You'll never lose me." He sealed her mouth once more with a gentle kiss.

He raised himself and gazed down at her, his expression filled with the same longing as before. "Will I ever be able to take away that serious look?" he asked, bending over her and kissing her eyes. "Even when you smile I see it."

She wanted to tell him how she felt but couldn't. For the first time in her life she wanted to belong to someone, yet she was still frightened of giving herself totally to him. Her lips trembled and he placed his fingers against her mouth as if reading her thoughts.

"You're more than I ever dared dream," he said quietly. "I'm going to have to teach you to trust me."

Her hand brushed through his tousled hair. "Where have I heard that before?"

He cradled her in his arms, and she felt him grow hard against her bare hip. He laughed softly. "At this rate, we may have to set up housekeeping here."

"I should leave now," she said, placing her hand on his. She didn't trust the emotions that ran through her.

"Why? Do you have plans for the day?"

"You know I do."

"Break 'em."

She shook her head, smiling. "You're a fine one to say that. I've been sleeping in the enemy camp, and when I appear in the committee room today, they'll know."

"Know what?"

She leaned over him and traced her fingers down his bare chest. "That you set off sparks in me that won't go out until the next century."

"You don't have to show up," he said. "The whole thing's a farce, anyway."

"Is it now?" She wasn't ready for the same old battle, she thought. Not now; not when he felt so good.

"You're thinking of Senator Glidden and me. Forget it. I didn't pull any strings with him. He was my brother-in-law for five years, and when the marriage broke up, we stayed friends. The meeting with him was pure old boy stuff. His son is my nephew and I think he still loves my sister."

"I'm learning about you in bits and pieces," she said. "I didn't know you had a sister."

"Sisters with bad marriages," he commented. "It's a national epidemic."

"You were right about Dan," she said slowly.

"I heard."

She looked at him hard. "How did you . . . ?"

"Not much happens around the station that I don't know."

She sat up and pushed herself back against the pillow. Sara wouldn't have said anything, so how—of course, Amy at the reception desk, perhaps even listening in on her phone call to Bobbie. Amy, gathering material for her writing class. Amy, who might have passed on the information to Casey just to make points with him. Well, well, well, life offered lots of surprises.

"It isn't a bad marriage," she said slowly. "They're two upwardly mobile people who are frightened to death of slipping back a notch, compounded with a teenager who thinks—excuse me, knows—the world revolves around her, and you have a lot of shattered nerves. It'll be okay. They're talking, and Dan is going for counseling." She smiled.

"I'm impressed," he said, and then he added, "I gather that's what inspired the program about runaways."

"You're on the ball, Casey."

"The program you think will change the world."

She turned to him and noted the small, self-assured smile on his face. "Just a small portion of it, Casey. Thanks to you I've had to ask Drew Berkeley to noise the project about."

"Ah, Drew Berkeley." Then he laughed, and reached for her. "Ten minutes with you in an upright position, Garrett, and we head for the boxing gloves. Come here."

She let his hand rest on her arm and felt the warmth seep through her, but the smile she gave him was deadly. "Casey, you're the most man I've ever met, but I've bought and paid for a room here, and right now I'm going to go use it. I'll see you at the hearing."

"I've said my piece at the hearing," he told her, returning her smile. "I stayed overnight because I had every intention of making love to you." He pulled her over him. "I'm in no hurry to get back to New York."

She let his mouth stray over hers and returned his kiss as though it were a long draught to a dying man. In some ways, it was. She would ease herself away after a while and go back to her room. There she would shower and try to wash away the scent of him. She had to, or she would go mad for love of him.

She'd attend the FCC hearing and have her say, putting her hope for the station on hold. If only she could predict the future... But she couldn't, and that was that. If Channel Eight wanted her, she'd have to accept and be happy about it.

One day she'd pick up the newspaper or Sheila would call her, and she'd find out what the FCC had decided. Meanwhile, she'd say what she had to in defense of serious programming, and then fly back to New York. There she'd bury herself in what she wanted to do more than anything in the world—see her program on runaways set

fire to New York and show Casey that her program did
mean something and life wasn't all kisses and laughs.

In a way, they were what she expected—scared youngsters with sweet faces, making a great show of bravado.
Articulate about why they had run away, they seemed
dazed about what had happened to them since and what
expectations they had for their future.

Four girls, two boys, all in their mid-teens with stories
to tell in pathetically young voices that Julie hoped would
galvanize the city's administration. Annie had short
bleached-white hair that stood out at all angles, wore too
much makeup and had the look of a punk rock star. Mark
looked underfed with his blotched face and bright-orange
ski jacket. Dawn was plump with long black hair, a great
wad of chewing gum in her right cheek. Jimmy was handsome, with a shy, silly smile that made him endearing, although they had taken a long, sharp blade away from him
not fifteen minutes before. Sandy, a blonde, had a bow-
shaped mouth painted bright red and a nervy look in her
wide blue eyes that belied her high IQ. Serious Millie was
a young black girl with hair carefully patterned in neat
cornrows.

For once, as they settled around the studio table, Julie
didn't feel the expected rise of panic. Father Halloran,
sitting opposite, a great, friendly presence, seemed to hold
an umbrella of goodwill over them.

"Just don't swoosh up close to the mike," Julie warned
them. "Every little sound is picked up." They giggled and
practiced drinking from the cans of soda that Sara offered them.

Then Julie gave them last-minute instructions and com-
plimented them on how cool they all seemed. She ad-

usted her headset. The engineer in the control booth nodded and she was on the air.

"This is Julie Garrett of *Night Talk*, and tonight we're beginning a week-long series of programs about runaways. It's a topic that's touched many of us one way or another. Whether a youngster has run away for a day or a year, or forever, the very act changes our lives irrevocably." She paused and looked at Sara in the control booth, getting a reassuring smile, then went on. "We're going to cover a broad range of topics. Why they run away, what happens to them, how parents can read the first signs of dissatisfaction in the parent-child relationships, where they can help. We'd like to try to solve some specific problems, open up others to the listening audience, and perhaps wake up some sleeping city officials."

Julie sensed rather than saw some movement in the control booth. She looked up and found that Casey Philips had come in. He was standing at the back, hands in pockets, his expression serious. Normally his presence would have rattled her but not now, not when she felt so much right was on her side.

Father Halloran gave her a gentle smile and Julie went on quickly. "We have six youngsters, all runaways, with us tonight. Of these, four are from the city, two from out of town. They promised to come to WRBZ if we would give them complete anonymity. We made that promise and we're going to stick to it, which means we've changed their names for the duration of the program. I'd also like to point out that radio tends to change the sound of one's voice, so I'm going to ask you to refrain from calling us and claiming that your son or daughter is on our program because you recognize the name and voice." Julie herself did not know their names. She had been insistent about that, and Father Halloran had agreed with her.

"With our six," she went on, "is Father Dave Halloran, director of Halloran House, a place that takes in youngsters on the run. He knows more about these kids and their problems, I believe, than any man alive. Now every night this week, we'll have runaways on the program along with experts and parents who have been through the problem. So please call with questions or comments and remember that the kids are here to present the general problem, not to address specific ones. Bear with us."

As she read the telephone number, Julie noted that Casey had taken a seat near the door to the control booth and that his face was in shadow. For a moment she felt a faint rush of anger, as though he had no right first to thwart her and then take a proprietary interest, but her anger came and went rapidly. With or without him, the show—her life—must go on. She adjusted her headset once again and dug in.

She was drenched. The two hours had raced by and suddenly Sara had signaled her that she had to wrap it up. Julie, with all her experience and sophistication, had been stunned and touched as the kids revealed all they had been through. Parental neglect and abuse, failure at school, the feeling that there was no one they could trust, the descent into drugs and alcohol. They had escaped from one terror only to run headlong into another kind. It ran the gamut and their only hope was to encounter someone like Father Halloran with his home for runaway children.

Sara, in the control booth, was pumping her hands together in a congratulatory gesture as Julie told her li

:ners the program was over. Casey had disappeared before
:e last commercial. All through the program she had been
ware of his sitting in the control booth without moving.
!alfway through, the knowledge had hit her that she
anted him there, needed him there as though he were the
)ck *she* could lean against.

Father Halloran got to his feet and put out his hand.
Well, I think my friends here behaved themselves very
ell,'' he said, beaming at her.

"They did, indeed," she said.

The kids awkwardly got to their feet. "Yeah, it was
kay," said Jimmy.

"Do you think I could come back sometime?" Millie
sked diffidently.

"Of course," Julie said, giving her a spontaneous hug.

Sara came into the studio. "It was a terrific program,
ulie, but your warning to parents not to call about these
ids didn't mean a thing."

"How many?" Julie asked. She put her arm through
Iillie's and walked with her to the door. "Come on, I've
ot a whole carton of sandwiches and cookies in my of-
ice. I figured you'd need something to eat for a job well
one."

"What would you say to fifty?" Sara's voice sounded
ehind her as they went out the door.

"Fifty!" Julie stopped dead and turned around. "From
ne metropolitan area? There has to be something wrong."

"Oh ye of little faith," Sara said. "You have listeners
nd the switchboard is jammed with them telling us that
hey're the parents of one of these kids."

Father Halloran came up to them. "Did you get names
nd addresses?"

"I did," Sara said. "I said you'd get back to them, bu they're clamoring. They didn't like the 'we'll get back t you' part at all. I have visions of them storming the sta tion tomorrow, Julie. I hope we haven't bitten off mor than we can chew."

"Just send them on to me," Father Halloran said "We'll handle it the best way we can."

Millie, with Julie's arm still tucked through hers, said a scared voice to the priest, "You won't tell, will you?"

"No, Millie," he said kindly, "we won't tell. You won' have to go home until you and your parents are ready."

It was seven o'clock that morning, however, before Ju lie learned the full extent of what they had done.

Her telephone rang, waking her from a deep sleep. Th woman's voice at the other end said at once, "I know yo have an unlisted number, but that didn't make any differ ence to me since I work for the telephone company. Tha was my daughter Dawn on your show last night."

A dozen calls followed, but Julie had enough sense afte the third call to switch on her answering machine.

She tried several times to reach Father Halloran, but th lines to Halloran House were busy and for a while all th telephone lines to the station were tied up. She was begin ning to feel spooked. She was dressed and ready to leav for Halloran House, when she decided to check out the re of the calls that had come in that morning.

Casey's voice was terse and annoyed. "Check in with m first thing."

"Is that your last word on the subject?" she asked th taped voice. Not the first thing, not the second thing, no the third thing, she told herself. It was going to be a bus day. She hadn't spoken with Casey since leaving him in th hotel room in Washington, and she wasn't about to star now. She wanted no diversions, no lectures, no advice. She felt somehow as though she were on a roller coaster, on the long down side, coming in for a stomach-squeezing stop.

Sara called, as well. "You're up early and out," the message stated. "Good for you. I'm on my way into the station. I think we're going to be a little swamped with distraught parents. One of my friends called, imagine! Her daughter's gone and she never even told me. See you soon."

There was a message to call Father Halloran, but his line was busy when she tried it. Her sister had also called with a quick message in a voice that held some hope. "Lindy heard the program, and so did Dan. He really wants to work things out Julie. Thanks for being there when Lindy needed you. When we all needed you."

There were two more messages from the woman who insisted Dawn was her daughter. Julie called the telephone company, explained that her unlisted number had been found out and requested a new one. No, she had no idea how half of New York City seemed to know her unlisted number.

By the time Julie stepped out of the cab at Halloran House, she had gone through the early afternoon editions of the papers. Drew had been hard at work on her behalf. There was a small breaking news item in the *Post*, and one in the *Times*, both about jammed telephone switchboards because of the program.

"There you are." Father Halloran found her in the hallway as she pushed her way through an unexpected crowd of people waiting to see him. He rushed her back to his office. "Good Lord, the entire city was up last night listening to your program," he said, looking pleased.

Julie was a little nonplussed. "Father, I know what the problem is, and even the figures, but all of a sudden it seems as if every kid in the metropolitan area has run away from home."

He smiled ruefully. "What it shows is that parents care and they want their kids back."

She thought of Lindy. There were all kinds of problems, and not many of them would be solved so rationally. "This is just the beginning, isn't it?"

"But a beginning. We need beginnings, Julie," he said. "I feel like the kindly old philosopher, but if we could match half a dozen kids with their parents with a promise to talk and understand, wouldn't that be something?"

"It would be something, all right."

After working out the details for that night's program with Father Halloran, Julie took a cab to the station. Ordinarily she would have made it a long, pleasant walk across town, but she had an inkling that the station was in for its share of visitors too.

She wasn't far wrong. A glimpse through the heavy plate-glass windows in the lobby of Graff Towers confirmed her suspicion. There must have been close to two dozen people milling around the reception desk. From the looks on their faces, she knew they were out for blood and wondered how the guard was dealing with it. She'd call him from her office and ask him to send them to Halloran House. She went around the corner to the side entrance and took the freight elevator to the forty-ninth floor.

She went quickly into her office and found Sara there talking quietly on the telephone. She hung up after a few more words.

"They're thinking of calling the gendarmes," Sara said at once, scarcely looking up at her. "The phone's been ringing nonstop all morning. Messages piled up to here."

"Why don't they go to Halloran House?" Julie remarked.

"They figured you're the one with the program and the pull with their kids. Anyway, I told the guard to give them the address of Halloran House, and that you're out for the afternoon."

"Sara," Julie said, flopping into her chair, "you're years wiser than I am. How the devil are we going to handle this?"

"Being years wiser," Sara began—then the telephone interrupted her. "Casey at the bat," she said. "He wants you in his office, pronto."

Julie rapidly got to her feet and went over to the door. "He has a genius for timing." Washington had never happened, it seemed. Her body aching for his was mere foolishness. *You're my lover,* he had said. *I love you,* he had said. She felt as if the words had been imprinted on her brain.

Julie dawdled at the door to his office, and then when someone came walking down the corridor, she felt obliged to push the door open. "Casey called," she told his secretary.

"Go right in. The deck's clear."

"Swell." Still, she hesitated for a moment once again, then straightened her shoulders and marched in.

He was at his window, his back to her. "Casey?"

"Sit down."

"I'm not interested in sitting down."

He turned around and for a moment his eyes flickered over her. Then he said in a tone that was carefully neutral, "Graff wants to see you. He's splitting a gut."

"Good, maybe he'll lose a little weight."

"You're about to lose a lot more than that, Julie."

She stood facing him, aware of the unexpressed anger in his face, the way his muscles seemed to tighten.

"What is he going to do? String me up? You can tell me, Casey. As a matter of fact, I'd rather hear it from you."

He came around his desk and took her arm, yet after a moment dropped it as if he'd been burned. "There's a wonderfully smug look on your face like a bomber who lights the fuse and watches it all blow away. They want the names of the kids, Julie. Graff wants the names of the kids. You're going to have to produce them and that's all you need to know."

"What? Over my dead body. We promised those kids anonymity." She didn't have the names and she realized now that she could never admit it, not to Casey, not to Norbert Graff.

"You don't give a damn about the position you've put me in," he said. "I was committed to giving you full rein over your program until your contract was up. All you've done is bring the whole city down on the station. Graff wants your blood."

"I gave my word," she said tightly, "and I'm sticking to it, no matter what you or Graff wants." She took a step back, wanting more space between them. He was in a tight spot and she was sorry for that, sorry for what might spell the end of their relationship.

Until that moment Julie had never realized quite how alone she was. She had asked for unfettered authority, and had used it. She had no one now who stood to gain or lose as much as she. No one, not Father Halloran, not Sara, and not Casey, could offer her advice. It was her decision alone.

"Graff is out for blood," Casey went on. "Between the jabs that L.O.W. has been giving the company, and now this, you're making their public relations program a sham. You, Julie Garrett. When Norbert Graff hears your name, he emits a low growl. They're going to walk all over your contract, Julie."

"I'm not giving up that list. It's not mine to give, and I don't give a damn about my contract."

A satisfied light gleamed in his eye for an instant and then vanished. He walked over to his telephone and pushed Graff's extension. "We're on our way, Mr. Graff."

"Come on, soldier," he said in a softened tone to Julie, "the big boss wants to see you right now. I'll keep you company and make sure he doesn't come down on you too hard."

"Casey, I can take care of myself. Haven't you learned that already?"

He grinned and pulled her over, wrapping his arms around her. "I learned it the hard way. I'm coming with you. Right now I'm not your lover; I'm your friendly station manager."

"I got into it by myself and I can get out of it the same way. I don't need you putting words in my mouth, Casey."

"Let's go," he said, moving her toward the door. "I'm an old protector of my rear, Julie; you ought to know that. I'm not on anybody's side but Casey Phillips's."

"I wonder." She walked ahead of him out to the elevator. "I don't want you for or against me, Casey, as a matter of fact. I'll work this thing out on my own."

"Being alone is not always a virtue."

"Today it's a virtue."

There were several people gathered around the reception desk; irate parents, she guessed, who had somehow gotten past the guard downstairs. She shook her head imperceptibly as the receptionist was about to call to her. This was not the time to deal with a dozen clamoring adults.

"Is that Julie Garrett?" She heard the audible question posed once or twice as they waited for the elevator. It came to a stop and she stepped inside with Casey. "I'll take care of them as soon as this business with Norbert Graff is over," she stated, hoping that her voice sounded more confident that she felt.

Norbert Graff was less than pleasant. "Well, you've opened a fine can of worms," he said at once, when they came into his office. He didn't invite them to sit down.

"Why can't you leave this sort of thing to the do-gooders?" he asked in a querulous voice. "Heaven only knows the town is filled with them. These people are clamoring for one thing only, Julie. I want them off my back. I want you to give them the names of the kids you had on last night."

Julie calmly sat down and crossed one leg over the other. She knew that her heart was beating unnecessarily fast, and that this face-off with the head of Graff could be the most important in her life. She couldn't afford to blow it. "They know the way to Halloran House," she said. "I'll remind them of the fact just as soon as I leave here."

"And they'll go. Just that simple?" Graff came over to her and for a moment hovered over her chair. She thought with something amounting to amusement, that he wanted to shake her out of her complacency.

"I'm not giving up the names. If it's to Father Halloran's benefit to do so, then it's up to him."

Graff stormed to the other end of his office, and then stopped to relight the cigar he held. "I've had him on the phone. He claims he gave his word to these kids and his word is sacred—sacred to a bunch of scarecrows. They don't know what the word means."

"My word is sacred, too, Mr. Graff. What are we arguing about? We promised these kids anonymity. Father Halloran is going to work everything out, but not under pressure. At least one good thing has come out of this—Halloran House is getting publicity, which will mean funding."

"You should be worrying about your own paycheck," Graff said.

Julie stood up. "Is that what you wanted to see me about? My contract?" she asked coldly.

"I want that reception room emptied," Graff told her in a hard, barely controlled tone. "I've already heard from every newspaper in town, and I had to dodge the TV cameras first thing this morning. A bunch of damn parents who can't control their own kids, and they've called the press down on me." He grunted and chomped down on his cigar. "No, not on me, on you, Garrett. You're going to take the fall on this one."

"I never said I wouldn't—" she began, but he interrupted her.

"I've got a dozen companies from coast to coast making profits for Graff, and this crummy station is giving me more trouble than all of them put together. I've half a mind to unload it right now." He looked sharply over at Casey as if for his reaction. "I don't have to wait for the FCC to tell me what to do."

"We're all in this together, Norbert." Casey's tone was quiet and reasonable. "Don't dump on Julie because it's been that kind of day. She gave her word about these kids, and she'll have to keep it."

Julie turned to him in open surprise. He was on her side.

Graff's eyes had narrowed. "Watch your feet, Phillips. If you step on my toes, I'll have you drummed out of here so fast you won't have time to pick up your shaving kit."

A look of cold fury passed over Casey's face, but Graff gave him no time to respond. His eyes fastened once again on Julie, although she scarcely heard his words. Casey had no choice now but to leave the station and it was all her fault. "As for your program tonight," Graff told her, "I'm afraid that we're going to have a little trouble between the station and our transmitter station in New Jersey. What a pity to have to replace it with piped-in music. I wouldn't count on it being fixed until Saturday morning. Good day, Ms. Garrett." He went behind his desk and sat down, picking up his telephone receiver so that she couldn't interrupt him.

Stunned, she watched as Casey went briskly across the room to take the receiver out of Graff's hand. "Listen to me," he said in a voice that was new to Julie. "You're not going to shut down the transmitter. You'll only be calling down more trouble on the station."

Graff started to say something, then changed his mind when he saw the expression on Casey's face.

"That program airs tonight, tomorrow night, the night after that, and ends on Friday," Casey said in the careful tones one might use for a child. He kept his hand on the phone. "I'm the station manager and I decide what goes on the air." He lifted his hand and for a moment stood ooking thoughtfully down at Graff. Then he turned around and said to Julie, "Let's go."

"Just a minute," Graff said. "No one leaves this office until I say so."

She heard Casey give a raw laugh when Graff went on, 'I'm going to give you a chance to change your act, Ca-ey. I've had my head turned by a pretty face once or twice nyself."

Julie colored, but felt Casey's hand on her arm, and lidn't move.

"I can understand your taking all this personally," Graff said in a new, cajoling tone to Julie, "seeing as how you've had trouble in your own family. But I wonder whether you'd be holding back if it were your sister out here."

Julie blanched at his remark and looked involuntarily at Casey, but was met with a faint shake of the head. No, she wouldn't have been so firm about withholding Lindy's name. In fact, her sister was the first person she had called. It was something to think about. She turned without an-swering and went over to the door. She heard Graff snort and then bellow something into his telephone.

Casey followed her out. "Thanks for sticking up for ne," Julie said quietly, then asked, "Will the program go on tonight?"

"It will."

Julie stopped. They were in the empty corridor now, doors closed on all sides. For a moment she marveled at the silence of offices now that computers had replaced the clicking of typewriters. Too silent, as though it were in-habited by robots. Then somewhere, as if to rebut her fancy, a door slammed, and simultaneously a telephone rang. She turned to Casey and hesitantly put her hand on his arm.

"Casey, believe me, I didn't mean to put you on the spot. I never expected you to stick up for me in there." She hesitated for a moment. "Will you lose your job?"

"Don't worry. I'll stick around long enough to see that your program airs until the end of the week."

"That's not what I was asking, Casey."

"Like you said before, sometimes you have no choice." But there was something final in his tone and she knew it was no use keeping him there talking. She had forced a confrontation between Casey and Graff, and Casey had paid the price.

"What will you do?"

He reached out and for an instant let his fingers drift the length of her face. "Get off the fast track for a while."

Take me with you, she wanted to say but didn't. For a long moment they stood looking at one another. "Are you angry with me?"

"Julie, you once accused me of trying to run your life. Funny how it's worked out the other way around." He bent over and kissed her lips lingeringly, and then after giving her a long, searching look, walked quickly away.

It was two-thirty in the morning. Friday, no, Saturday. Well, no matter. She would be on a daytime schedule from now on, her biological clock like everyone else's. She looked around her tiny office with something resembling nostalgia. *Night Talk* was over finally, irrevocably, and the week had ended with a bang. There had been plenty of media coverage, the kids had kept their anonymity and Halloran House had found two new corporate sponsors.

The last of the kids had been tucked under the protective wing of Father Halloran, and her program on runaways was over and done with, a fitting finish to her years of *Night Talk*. And what now? She had the answers, but they lacked excitement, somehow.

She ought to call a cab and go home. Instead, Julie laid her head on her arms and closed her eyes. She should be happy. Her agent, calling her with the good news about the job at Channel Eight, had told her so. Sara, kissing her on the cheek and insisting they meet for lunch weekly, had told her so.

She hadn't seen Casey again. She hadn't even tried. The look he had given her in the corridor outside Graff's office had been enough. It's all over, the look had said. You're too much trouble.

Still, it was amazing that they could occupy the same space and yet not once run into each other. That he was physically there she had no doubt and she was certain he was responsible for her program staying on the air.

There was a soft knock at her office door, then it opened and Vic Cooper peered in. "Figured you'd still be around," he said. "Can I come in?"

She looked up gratefully, realizing she might have been asleep for a moment. "Oh sure, Coop. What are you doing here at this time of night, anyway?"

He came in carrying two containers of coffee and put one on her desk. "Figured you'd need something hot to drink about now. Some fan laid a lot of old seventy-eights on me and I've been taping them. You know me; I just begin to wake up around this time of night."

She put her hand around the container and felt its warmth. "Thanks, Coop. I've been thinking about calling a cab and going home, but I just didn't have the energy.'' She took a sip. It tasted acrid, of cardboard and too much sugar, yet she loved it. It was WRBZ and *Night Talk* and everything that was over.

Coop pulled up Sara's chair and straddled it. "Hey, kid, I'm gonna miss you, but congratulations about Channel Eight. One thing I can say about you, you're going out with all flags flying. There was enough media coverage of that whole event to fill your scrapbook, wasn't there?"

"The best thing was that I think we made some parents address the issue. We woke them up too much for a while there, but that's all worked out. Father Halloran said he was able to match a couple of kids with their families. Isn't that fantastic?"

He reached across the desk and patted her hand. "You do good work, Julie. Glad of the Channel Eight gig?"

"Yes, of course."

"Hey, put a little oomph in that remark!" He stood up. "Come on, let's have a celebratory drink at Harris's."

She laughed and shook her head. "Sara wanted to take me home with her for a drink, too, but I said no, I just wanted to be alone."

"It's an order," Vic said. "Grab your bag and let's go."

She sighed. "I have to clean up. There's a whole bunch of things I ought to take with me. My Rolodex, for one. It's mine."

He reached over and grabbed the Rolodex. "I'll carry it."

She sighed once again. He was right. She shouldn't go back to her apartment, not quite yet. There was a lot of unwinding to do. "Right. Sara can send everything if I don't want to come back." She got up and went around her desk, past Coop, to the door. "So long, old office

thout a window. So long, old teddy bear, aspidistra, and
ilodendron. See you...never.''

It was a weekend night and Harris's was crowded, so
ey stood at the bar. The view of the upright piano was
ocked, but Julie saw Sammy Roy sitting at a table op-
site the stand.

The song was "Stormy Weather"—and Julie knew at
ice why Coop had brought her there.

"He's playing, isn't he?" she said simply.

Color suffused Coop's face and he smiled at her.
You're quick. I'll say that much for you, Julie.''

She felt a long wave of warmth rush through her. Coop
uched her arm briefly as if to hold her back. But she
ouldn't have run, couldn't have if she'd wanted to. The
usic seemed to go on forever and she listened to it with
osed eyes. When it was over, the set ended and suddenly
 was standing over her.

"See you, Coop, and...thanks," he said.

Julie didn't even notice when Coop left them.

"Come on," Casey said, taking her arm and leading her
it the door. "Time to go home." The night was warm
d they went over to the curb, the light from the club en-
loping them in a soft, warm glow.

"My Rolodex," she said suddenly.

"Was that what Coop was carrying as if it contained the
own Jewels?"

She laughed tremulously, knowing that her laugh held
 e makings of a sob.

"Shall we find a cab or walk?" Casey asked.

"We'll never get a cab at this hour. Let's walk. Home,
 e long way around."

"Mmm," he said, linking his arm through hers, a
lacing their fingers tightly together, "wonder if I can p
those words to music?"

"I don't think you have to, they're already music. O
Casey," she cried. "I thought it was all over between us

He looked down at her, his face so close she could fe
his breath on her cheek. "Now where did you get th
idea?"

She stopped in the middle of the pavement. "Where d
I get that idea? From the absolute finality of your wor
on Tuesday. How's that for starters? Our being in the san
place at the same time all week without once commu
cating."

"Kept tabs on me, did you?"

"Oh," she groaned in mock anger, "I didn't have t
There's a different feel to the place when you're there."

A look of boyish satisfaction crossed his face at h
words. "Well, that's the best thing I've heard in a lo
time, Julie." He bent over and pressed his lips lingering
against hers. "But I didn't want to call you. I needed tin
to think about where I was going," he added. "I thoug
I was a man on my way up and suddenly up didn't loc
quite as good as I thought."

"What looks good, then?" she asked softly, scarce
aware of holding her breath, knowing that her whole li
hinged on his next words.

"You. In my dreams, in reality, and very definitely in n
future. It's all the rest I still have to come to terms with.

His words were spoken so casually, she understood
last that he had always loved her, and that she had r
fused to see it.

They stopped at the corner and waited once again,
they had that first night, for the Walk light to flash on.

ne car came by, a small sports model, its low rumble
ınctuated by a funny little tick in the motor.

"I've got some composing on my mind, Julie. It's pos-
ıle I might want to take some time off and play some
usic locally."

"And your job at WRBZ?"

He smiled without answering her question. "What
⸱out your job?"

"Come on, you've got spies everywhere. You know I've
ft the station and I'm going with Channel Eight."

"Then again, my options are open," he told her.
There's a station for sale in Pennsylvania, and I was
ınking..."

She put her hands on his lips. "Don't even say it."

"I'll put the idea on hold. I want you, Julie," he said.
For good, for keeps, forever. Do you think you could
ve a jazz man?"

She threw her arms around his neck. "I loved a razz-
atazz man, no reason why I wouldn't love a jazz man."

His lips silenced her for a long moment. "Think we'll
ake it?"

"Is that a proposal?" she asked.

His lips held hers. A cab pulled up and the driver
ɔnked his horn. Julie pulled away. "Hey, a cab at three
 the morning! That's an omen, Casey, surely it's an
nen!"

ᗡ Silhouette Desire

COMING NEXT MONTH

LOVEPLAY—Diana Palmer
When Edward McCullough set out to write his new play, he never intended for his old flame, Bett, to act in his cast. But Bett was determined to convince him that their love was still in the script.

FIRESTORM—Doreen Owens Malek
Jason was haunted by the accident that had left him widowed. But then he met Alison, his son's teacher, who taught him not to let the darkness in his past color their chance for a bright future.

JULIET—Ashley Summers
Determined to rebuild her family's fortune, Juliet was going to need some help. Cord was a Romeo in disguise. But could he save her from ruin and win her for himself?

SECRET LOVE—Nancy John
By day they were enemies, rival experts for the world's two most famous auction houses. But by night, Paula and Quinn savored a love that knew no allegiances.

FOOLISH PLEASURE—Jennifer Greene
Passion still flared between Stephanie and Alex long after their divorce— and their son was bent on playing matchmaker. Steph wasn't going to get close to Alex again, but how could she deny an undeniable love?

TEXAS GOLD—Joan Hohl
When model Barbara Holcomb arrived to assist her elderly aunt, she found herself in the midst of a real Texan manhunt. Her partner in pursuit was Ranger Thackery Sharp, but it was soon unclear who was pursuing whom!

AVAILABLE THIS MONTH:

CHOICES
Annette Broadrick

NIGHT TALK
Eve Gladstone

KNOCK ANYTIME
Angel Milan

PLAYING THE GAME
Kathleen Korbel

YESTERDAY AND TOMORROW
Candice Adams

CATCHING A COMET
Ann Hurley

If you're ready for a more sensual, more provocative reading experience...

We'll send you
4 Silhouette Desire novels
FREE
and without obligation

Then, we'll send you six more Silhouette Desire® novels to preview every month for 15 days with absolutely no obligation!

When you decide to keep them, you pay just $1.95 each ($2.25 each in Canada) *with never any additional charges!*

And that's not all. You get FREE home delivery of all books as soon as they are published and a FREE subscription to the Silhouette Books Newsletter as long as you remain a member. Each issue is filled with news on upcoming titles, interviews with your favorite authors, even their favorite recipes.

Silhouette Desire novels are not for everyone. They are written especially for the woman who wants a more satisfying, more deeply involving reading experience. Silhouette Desire novels take you *beyond* the others.

If you're ready for that kind of experience, fill out and return the coupon today!

Silhouette 💛 Desire®

Silhouette Books, 120 Brighton Rd., P.O. Box 5084, Clifton, NJ 07015-5084